Blood
Brothers

Also by Michael Schiefelbein
from Alyson Books

VAMPIRE VOW

Blood
Brothers

By Michael Schiefelbein

alyson books
los angeles | new york

© 2002 BY MICHAEL SCHIEFELBEIN. ALL RIGHTS RESERVED

MANUFACTURED IN THE UNITED STATES OF AMERICA.

THIS TRADE PAPERBACK ORIGINAL IS PUBLISHED BY ALYSON PUBLICATIONS,
P.O. BOX 4371, LOS ANGELES, CALIFORNIA 90078-4371.
DISTRIBUTION IN THE UNITED KINGDOM BY TURNAROUND PUBLISHER SERVICES LTD.,
UNIT 3, OLYMPIA TRADING ESTATE, COBURG ROAD, WOOD GREEN,
LONDON N22 6TZ ENGLAND.

FIRST EDITION: OCTOBER 2002

02 03 04 05 06 **a** 10 9 8 7 6 5 4 3 2 1

ISBN 1-55583-729-8

CREDITS
• COVER PHOTOGRAPHY BY JEFF PALMER.
• COVER DESIGN BY MATT SAMS.

One

Juan Ramón

Bloodshed.

That's what I thought of that first day as I walked from the train station toward the medieval city. How the hell could I not? Enough blood had been spilled in Toledo—by Christians, Moors, Visigoths, and Romans—to turn the muddy Tajo River as red as a cardinal's robe.

Just before me on a bluff brooded the Moorish Castle Servando. The crenellated towers had seen flesh cut and pierced and burned in the name of Allah, Christ, and Spain. Blood fused with the dust and mortar and ancient stone of not only the castle but the town awaiting me just over the Alcántara Bridge.

Blood in the towers and tiled roofs, blood in the narrow streets winding through the clutter of shops and open markets, blood even in the cloisters. All the blood in the whole walled city cried out to me.

I followed a maze of narrow streets through the town, stopping for directions at an outdoor café. The willowy young waiter eyed my habit shyly, stuttering as he explained where to find the monastery. I thought to myself what a nice fuck he would be.

"Bring me a glass of your house red wine," I said.

"*Sí*, Padre." He nodded obediently and trotted off.

I set my satchel and suitcase on the ground near a table with an umbrella and took a seat.

It was hard to believe the time had come.

Continuity was the reason for the delay. All the years at the Salesian home for boys, college studies at the University where I lived with the Salesian community, then seminary training and ordination—it was all of a piece. The long refectory tables; prayers of the Divine Office that punctuated the day; the small, scantily furnished cells.

Though in no way did I feel indebted to the Salesians, I'd never hated them like I'd hated the orphanage nuns in my earlier days. The Salesians didn't beat me with brushes or lock me in a closet or make me recite rosaries while the other inmates got fed. Their number never included a sadistic bitch like Sister Maria Rosario. She'd forced me to kneel for hours at a time, with my hands extended in front of me as though I were a prisoner of war. She'd gotten off on inventing details of my parents' murder, for which, she reminded me, I'd been responsible because I was evil in God's sight.

I'd cut out the rebelliousness fairly soon after arriving at the Salesian home for boys. Under its shelter came savvy. I learned to check my rage and discovered a means to eventually vent it once and for all. That's when I formed the master plan. I needed the tools the monks could give me—education, reputation, and, above all, resoluteness and the discipline to sustain that plan over many years until I could finally recover the untroubled sleep I used to enjoy before the murder.

"Here you are, Padre," the waiter lisped. He deposited the glass on the table clumsily, spilling a little on the white cloth. "I'm sorry."

"That's all right," I said, smiling.

I watched his tight round ass as he went to another table. Then, closing my eyes, I sipped my wine and took a deep breath before pulling three folders out of my satchel.

The first folder was thin. It contained handwritten descriptions and sketches of the two thugs who had killed my parents while a third man—their boss, Martin Esteban—stood by with me, a 7-year-old, in his iron grip. The sketches were based on what I remembered as I struggled to free myself from Esteban. But my memories were supplemented by the sometimes distorted, sometimes horrifyingly vivid views granted me in nightmare after nightmare. I'd revised the descriptions for a year after moving to the home for boys, then forced myself to stop before my hatred contorted them beyond usefulness.

One of the thugs was short and stocky. The sleeves of his blue shirt had been cut off from the shoulders, as if to free his muscular arms, one imprinted with a long tattoo of a cobra ready to strike. As the man straddled my mother, prone on her bedroom floor, and pinned back her arms, I had noted his stupid, excited eyes, recessed beneath the brow of a huge, ugly guard dog—a mastiff.

"I can, *que no?*" he had called to Esteban.

Esteban stood near the door, restraining me, while the second thug pressed his knee into the back of my father, face down on the mattress, and held a gun to his head. *He pressed his knee into the* left *side of my father's back*, I always mentally added whenever I reviewed the scene, *the side with the cracked ribs from a horseback riding accident the week before*. Papa had winced.

"Do the hell what you want," Esteban shouted at the mastiff. Then he commanded the other thug to finish the job on my father.

The only thing I noticed about Papa's murderer was his size: He was as big and muscular as an American football player.

A frantic chant started inside my head: *Watch out for Papa's ribs, watch out for Papa's ribs, his ribs, his ribs, his ribs*. My defenses kept the possibility of murder somewhere in a cloudy distance. *The left side, the left side, the left side. That trunk of a knee will break his ribs*.

My mother's screams distracted me for a moment. Then the shot came. The blood that sprayed from my father's head was the last image in my conscious mind.

The fatal bullet in my father's brain and my mother's rape and murder by a separate gun—these facts I'd pieced together from careless police chatter outside the door before the detective interviewed me.

My review of the police records years later, when I was a teenager, had confirmed these facts. They had also recalled to me the conclusions formed by the detective and his associates about the two thugs. Probably they were disgruntled factory hands at my father's Bilbaoan textile plant, paid enough pesetas for killing my parents to allow them to quit their jobs and drink the rest of their lives away. Probably they felt justified for political reasons, Basques striking out against a Nationalist oppressor.

The police report included my description of the two thugs: "one big man and one small one with a snake tattooed on his arm." But their names were missing. Carlos Castro and Umberto Entralgo. Names I had finally found printed under black and white police photographs. I'd studied hundreds of pages of photos—scowling, brooding, cold faces—until I'd come across the two forever etched in my memory.

The stupid-looking thug, my mother's rapist and murderer, was Carlos Castro. My father's killer, the hulking man with big features and wide-set eyes glaring at me in the photo, Umberto Entralgo.

Also missing from the police report was my identification of Esteban. This despite the fact that I clearly remembered reporting the information to the detective on the case: "It was Papa's partner, Señor Esteban," I'd said. "We've had him over for dinner." I also clearly remembered that the fat detective had glanced at another officer after he heard the words "Señor Esteban," and that they had left the room and then returned without another reference to my remark.

After making futile protests about the purged report 15 years ago, I'd recorded the details of the attack as I remembered it and begun investigating the matter myself.

I sipped my wine.

Placing aside my notes on the two thugs, I picked up the second folder. I thumbed through the news clippings in it, all about Esteban from the business and society sections of the newspaper. The headlines announced his accomplishments and wealth: "Tessuto España Inc. Expands," "Esteban Calls the Bluff of Striking Workers," "Esteban Opens Second Plant," "Christmas on Esteban's Yacht."

I examined the neatly clipped photos of Esteban, a handsome man with keen, dark eyes and an air of power stored just beneath his face. The photos showed him in a trim mustache and tailored suit shaking hands with board members, pounding a podium, laughing with Franco, touring his new factory.

Over the years, I had assumed that Esteban's motive for killing my father was to gain complete power over the company. My mother had been a decoy: In the event that uncorrupted investigators were on the case, her murder, along with my father's emptied safe and wallet, would support a robbery motive. But practical motive or not, Esteban's ruthlessness and arrogance—crystal clear in the photographs—made me believe the tycoon had prided himself, even taken cruel pleasure, in killing Ramón and Alicia Fuertes.

I opened the third folder now. It contained a simple pledge. I read it every day as a kind of reconsecration to the mission that defined my life. I'd written in a sort of code, in the unlikely event that my notes were discovered. I made my words sound like a spiritual diary: *Son is key to Father. Befriend Son. Inspect Father's house. Seek Devil's agents: Death and Destruction. Annihilation of Death and Destruction. Deliver Justice to Father.*

The son—that was Bernardo Esteban, Brother Bernardo, fellow Salesian. He was the reason I'd chosen the Monastery of Santo Domingo.

One of my news clippings reported Bernardo's grand

entrance into the order's high-school seminary 13 years before. I pulled out the article. "Son of Tycoon Martin Esteban Begins Training as Salesian," said the headline, above a photo of Esteban presenting the 14-year-old boy to the Salesian rector. Notable in the photo was the dissatisfaction in Esteban's eyes.

Two

Bernardo

I slipped my rosary under the sheets, wrapped it around the dangerous flesh.

My cell was warm for May, not a hint of draft through the single window, and the rosary's silver crucifix was cool against my scrotum. My eyes had adjusted to the scant light filtering in from the street lamps in the Plaza de Alfonso to the west of the monastery. I could make out the outline of my narrow bed, the sink in the corner of the cell, the desk, and my habit thrown over a chair.

So to concentrate I squeezed my eyes shut, summoned the smooth white body of the crucified Lord.

Sweat dripped from his armpits as he struggled to breathe in the heat of a noon sun. I wrapped my arms around his stained feet, tasted the metallic flavor of his blood. I pressed my chest, my belly, my thighs against the rough wood. The words of San Juan de la Cruz came to me... *Abandon yourself and forget yourself...laying your face on your Beloved, all things will cease...you'll go out from yourself, leaving your cares...forgotten among the lilies.*

My Beloved calmed the desires. I didn't touch myself after all, despite a fire that had spread from front to back as though I had mounted a flaming saddle—a fire set by a stocky delivery boy I'd glimpsed that day. The day before Juan Ramón came into my life.

When did my temptations begin?

I was just 14 when I entered the Salesian minor seminary in Madrid. What did I know then about lust? A buzzing feeling came to my groin and nipples when the captain of the soccer team let me ride him piggy-back style down the field. I got so hard I thought I would explode in my shorts. I knew it was more than the bouncing. I knew his musky, sweaty body, his smooth bare back explained the sensations. Partly. The flutters hit me even when he was several meters away, fully clothed, leaning back arrogantly against the stone wall around the seminary.

The first time my hand slipped down to my groin after lights out...the first release of the dammed up force...it terrified me. *It shouldn't feel good*, I told myself. And the battle began. I lined up every week at the confessional. I gave up sweets. I slept without a pillow. I had to mortify my flesh, embrace the crucified Lord.

Black gloom descended upon me after each warm explosion. I'd run to the chapel, kneel on the stone floor for an hour, my arms stretched straight out, my tear-filled eyes fixed on the stripped corpus crucified above the high altar. *O Cristo, O Dios, Perdoname!* I'd whisper over and over.

After confession in the morning and a new resolution to crucify myself with Christ, I bounced along piously, working hard at studies, concentrating on the ball instead of on thighs and calves during soccer practice, averting my eyes from bare buttocks and groins in the shower room. There was no problem to address. The word *maricon*—which my classmates tossed around to tease each other on the playing field—didn't apply to me. And what did it matter? Celibacy was celibacy whatever form temptations took.

In the first year or so of college seminary, my thinking stayed the same. And then one Saturday I took the subway to Figueroa.

Seminarians seemed to use the words *maricon* and *Figueroa* interchangeably. I had a burning desire to see this Madrid neighborhood full of homosexuals, and on a boring morning at my parents' house I walked like an automaton to the subway at Atocha Station off the Paseo del Prado.

I exited the train at Figueroa along with a parade of other men.

The neighborhood wasn't as seedy as I had imagined it to be. Brick buildings seemed neat, their shutters brightly painted. Shop owners were hosing the sidewalks. A group of old men played board games in a small plaza with a fountain. I even saw some college girls enter a bookstore and a middle-aged woman in pearls walking her poodle.

But when I turned down a side street, I saw more of what I'd expected. In front of a plate glass window with

CAFÉ FIGUEROA scrawled in pink across the surface, a knot of boys my age talked animatedly, their hands whisking over each other's arms and faces and backsides. They wore tight jeans and mesh shirts. Two of the boys with bleached hair held hands. One dark boy turned from the wind to light a cigarette and caught sight of me staring. He smiled, and I walked away.

Down the street I passed two or three more cafés and a club. The club's windows shook from the music inside, even at that hour. On the brick wall outside, advertisements were posted. Words, obscene and exciting, were sprayed across the posters: *dominante*, *activo*, *esclavo*, *pasivo*. How was it I already knew what they meant? *Lluvia dorado, tortura de polla y huevos*—I imagined a boy's uplifted face baptized with urine, testicles in the grip of a bearded man's teeth.

One poster displayed two muscular bare-chested men in leather shorts and boots. One straddled a chair while the other stood behind him and inserted a riding crop in the seated man's mouth. I got hard and very scared. I went home.

But all day I couldn't stop thinking of Figueroa, and that same night I went back and slipped into a bar called El Mojito. The beat of Latin music pulsed through bodies colliding on the dark dance floor. Bare torsos, low-slung jeans, arms flaying, the sights, the movement, the smell of sweat and cologne and smoke and yeasty *cerveza* drew me into the collective body. I drank three *cervezas*. I moved to the music in a tight dark corner.

And when a thick-necked man in a leather jacket took my hand, I followed him to a back room where several pairs of men were entwined. He kissed me. I had never been kissed. His tongue pushed through my lips and I sucked it as though it were the only nourishment that could keep me alive. His bushy moustache raked across my smooth skin. It smelled of tobacco. *Pobrecito*, he moaned in my ear when his hand found the swollen flesh in my pants. And then he dropped to his knees and his mouth caressed me, took me in. The movement was steady, rhythmic, as determined as a builder's hammering.

Cielos! This was heaven.

The guilt that followed was a new kind: not just a deep black pit, but a furious storm. There could be no innocent forgetting, no more cycles of penance and sweet oblivion. I was a *maricon*. Disordered, perverse. I could easily be a lost soul—now, now when priesthood was within sight. I had to stop even the fantasies. I had to replace one lust with another.

And so I immersed myself in the mysticism of San Juan della Cruz:

One dark night
Fired by love's urgent longings
Ah, the sheer grace!
I went out unseen...
Upon my flowering breast
Which I kept wholly for Him alone
There He lay sleeping, And I caressing Him
There in the breeze from the fanning cedars.

A few failures came—a curly-headed Basque classmate with no qualms about crawling into beds at night, an athletic novice who let me massage his muscles and more. But mostly I remained faithful to my Lover through college, novitiate, and theological studies. I pledged myself to Him in my final vows. Ordination would be the marriage of our souls.

All I had to do was stay faithful to my Lover until the day I had awaited for over 10 years.

Three
Juan Ramón

I found the Monastery of Santo Domingo nestled amid churches and crumbling mansions that had been converted to apartment buildings. It was a 15th-century structure of stone and brick. On the lower part of the facade, stone saints gawked from a series of niches on both sides of the entrance. On the upper part a row of miter-shaped windows rose to meet a filigreed cornice.

The entrance of the monastery wasn't in the open, which pleased me. My coming and going wouldn't be observed. But around the building I found that the chapel, which ran parallel to the facade, opened onto a bright plaza. The two stone spires gleamed in the May sun. *Too damned exposed*, I thought. Still, there wasn't much activity on the plaza, just a few vendors under the awnings near a fountain, and a small café.

I continued around the monastery, which would occupy a whole damned block in Madrid. The structure was standard: a square formed by four buildings with the chapel at the head. But the niches, filigree, and gothic windows created sublime lines and curves and shadows that transformed the simple design into something exotic. Back at the front I climbed the stone steps to the entrance and set down my suitcase and satchel.

One of the door's glass panes reflected my face. I've got my father's looks: a beak of a nose maybe, but good-looking over all—square jaw, high cheekbones, full lips in the center of a dark goatee, and eyes bold and hard enough to attract boys who want to be whipped into shape. According to my old novice master, my looks and hardness intimidated the other novices. Little did he know what forms intimidation could take in a dark cell.

I rang the bell. A dog barked inside. When a flabby red-headed monk in his fifties opened the door, a dingy white terrier bounded out and leapt up on my clean habit.

"*Que malo*, Sancho! Down, boy." The monk pulled the mutt down by the collar and commanded him to sit, which he did. "*Lo siento*, Padre—please forgive Sancho. He loves visitors. You must be Juan Ramón."

"Yes." I straightened the long scapular that fell down the front of my habit.

"Sancho and I have been waiting for you, haven't we, boy? I'm Brother Diego." The monk smiled, exposing a mouthful of broken yellow teeth. "Please, let me take your suitcase."

"Thanks, but I can handle it." Diego's friendliness and his boisterous mutt put me more on guard than usual. I hoped the porter wasn't typical of the residents at Santo Domingo.

Looking disappointed, Diego showed me into the dimly lit entrance hall. "Abbot Baroja is in the courtyard," he said, securing the latch. "It's this way." The dog barked and ran ahead. "Yes, Sancho," he called, "You know where we're going, don't you?"

We passed through the lofty foyer to a set of doors leading to the courtyard. I followed Diego through the cloister surrounding the bright garden, down a flight of stairs and past a fountain to the section of the courtyard closest to the chapel. There the abbot was petting Sancho, who had made straight for him.

"Here's our new man, Padre Baroja," Diego said.

"Very pleased to have you here, Father." Baroja, who had been kneeling to prune a rosebush, stood and removed his gardening gloves. He grabbed my hand with both of his. He was harmless looking, middle-aged, lanky, and browned from the sun. "Why don't we sit in the shade?" He motioned toward the cloister. "Thank you, Brother Diego." He nodded to the porter by way of dismissal.

Diego called to Sancho, who was drinking from the fountain. Master and dog made their way back to the porter's office.

I followed Baroja through the rose garden to a stone bench in the ground-floor section of the cloister. I was facing my first challenge—convincing the solicitous Father

Abbot that his new monk would be better off left alone.

"You should have called from the station. Someone could have come to get you." Perspiration beaded on Baroja's high broad forehead and bald scalp. He wiped the sweat off with the sleeve of his habit.

"I wanted to take in the city alone."

Baroja nodded as though he could understand such a desire. "And what do you think of Toledo so far?"

I thought a moment, my eyes on the fountain. I thought of the picturesque medieval haven I'd passed through on the way to Santo Domingo—a base of operation with easy access to Madrid but far enough from the city for my purposes. "It'll do."

Baroja laughed. The inside of his mouth glimmered with gold crowns. "Abbot González told me you were a model of detachment. You'd better be careful, or you'll end up novice master back in Salamanca."

Salamanca wasn't so bad, I thought. I'd taken my vows at the efficiently run monastery there, El Sacro Corazón. I'd been ordained a priest under González, who'd solicited a reassignment request from me as a matter of course—La Corazón having a surfeit of monks. González had welcomed my request to be sent to Toledo—as I had known he would, because except for *him*—Bernardo—the monks at Santo Domingo were drooling old men and the community was dwindling. "I suppose there are worse fates than Salamanca," I said.

"But as novice master?" Baroja smiled. "Not in my 30 years experience as a Salesian. The exuberance of novices can grate on one's nerves. Of course, I don't begrudge them their enthusiasm, knowing what lies ahead—street toughs, beggars, sick parishioners, the loneliness of celibate life. But it's something deeper than exuberance that fits one out for all that. Old fashioned stamina, I mean. Perhaps that's what I see in you?"

I kept my mouth shut.

Baroja took this as a cue to eye me with a sickening pity. "Abbot González has told me your road hasn't been an easy one. The loss of your parents, the Sisters' orphanage—before we Salesians were lucky enough to get you. I won't say that hardships make us better people. I've seen what the street does to boys. But you've stood up to them. Your academic performance at the University of Salamanca was exceptional. And during seminary training...well, Padre González tells me he's never seen such self-discipline."

"My parents were murdered, Father, my mother after being viciously raped." I spoke calmly. "I was 7 years old. I needed discipline to stay sane."

Baroja's expression turned serious, the pity evaporating. "One also needs the support of brothers. This community is your family now, Father. And as abbot I have a special obligation to you. Please call on me whenever you have need."

I reminded myself that men like Baroja must on principle thwart the sort of justice I had come to Toledo seeking. I also reminded myself that for every Baroja in the Church there was a Maria Rosario. The dog-faced Cerberus of a nun had whipped my bare ass when I wouldn't say my night prayers or when I wouldn't give prospective parents the time of day, not for all the ice cream and soccer games in the world.

Mandatory interview over, Baroja gave me a tour of the monastery. On the ground floor a spacious recreation hall opened out into the cloister where we'd chatted earlier. The room was divided into sitting areas with sofas and armchairs. There was a television, tables for games and reading, magazine racks, and a long counter for serving refreshments. Despite the cozy-looking furniture, the bare stone floors gave the hall a cold, grim feel. The rest of the ground floor was taken up by exercise rooms with showers and a number of locked storage rooms. On the main floor were large, dimly lit public rooms—a visitor's parlor, a refectory, a huge library, and offices for the porter and abbot.

The chapel was austere but stunning, its soaring vault formed by gothic arches rising like ribs along the two sides. Arches flanking the nave opened into side chapels. Light poured in through high windows, several of which were positioned along the sides and one in the organ loft above the entrance. In the chancel an intricate high altar rose almost to the ceiling, the niches filled with saints, a crucifix at the apex.

The monks' cells were on the second floor, reached by a staircase near the porter's office. *Where is his?* I wondered.

The furnishings in my cell—undoubtedly like all the other cells—were dark and spare against white plaster walls: a narrow bed covered with a gray blanket, a desk and chair, and a crucifix—the only wall adornment. A single miter-shaped window looked out on the narrow cobbled street I'd passed along when surveying the monastery. The street was lined with shops displaying brightly painted pottery, fruit, rugs, and other wares in front of their open doors. Above the rooftops, in the center of Toledo, loomed the cathedral's gothic tower, a cluster of points girdling a central spire.

Baroja nodded to the scuffed suitcase and satchel, which I'd dropped on the bed. "Do you have any more luggage?"

"No." I hoped he felt that he'd satisfied his role as host and would leave now.

"I'll let you settle in, then," he said, moving to the door. "The house schedule is in your desk. Evening prayer is at 7, then dinner. I'm afraid the evening meal is rather spare."

"If it's all right with you, I'll skip dinner and retire early."

"Of course. You must be tired. Oh, I've told Padre Simon to expect you at Santiago del Arrabal tomorrow. He's happy you are coming. The parishioners are excited too."

I forced a smile. Baroja had described my Toledo assignment during his tour. The old half-blind pastor of the church in the northern part of the city was in desperate need of an assistant.

The abbot opened the door, then turned back to me. "Remember, Father, I'm here if you need anything."

"That's kind of you."

Alone in my cell, I savored the moment that had finally arrived after 15 years of planning. I took off my sandals and the hot black habit and stretched out on the sagging cot in my underwear. A breeze flowed through the open window, which luckily faced east, shaded from the harsh afternoon sun. My mind went to the willowy waiter and I got hard. I imagined taking his ass, listening to him moan from pain then pleasure. I jerked off and cleaned myself up in the sink in the corner of the cell. Afterward I stretched out again, more relaxed.

The next morning, just after dawn, I sat in a choir stall among 20 monks in black hooded robes and sandals. The sun seeped through the stained glass opposite me. The image of a chalice, the window's centerpiece, glowed gold. The wafer suspended above the chalice was like a miniature white version of the sun.

The silent chapel was cool as a cave despite the heat already gathering outside. I closed my eyes and let my thoughts drift. The night before I'd dreamed I was sitting in a *café cantante*, where local flamenco singers performed. Instead of a woman dancer, the willowy waiter, naked from the waist up, stamped his boot heels and cried out the words of Federico García Lorca to the urgent strum of the guitar:

> *The cry of the guitar*
> *Begins.*
> *The crystal goblets of dawn*
> *Shatter.*
> *The cry of the guitar begins…*
> *It weeps for things distant.*
> *The sand of the hot south*
> *Aches for white camellias.*
> *The arrow without target,*
> *The evening without morning,*
> *And the first bird dead upon the branch,*
> *weep.*
> *Oh guitar—grievously wounded*
> *By five knives!*

The dream, the song, made me think of my life after the task was completed. Maybe I would go to the hot Andalusian south, to Seville perhaps. Maybe I would find a beautiful boy capable of facing life on its own terms. Maybe the fullness, the sensuality of the *juerga*, the flamenco session, would infuse our lives.

This sort of dream, this moment of quiet, were as much as I let myself think of the life after. Too much work needed doing first.

Across from me sat Bernardo Esteban. His close-set eyes were fixed earnestly on the curtained tabernacle at the base of the high altar. He could have been 17 instead of 27, he seemed so young and innocent. His skin was lighter than my olive skin and he was slightly built. The features of his heart-shaped face were delicate. I strained to see anything of the elder Esteban in the son—the volatility, the ruthlessness, the predatory charm. But no trace of them glimmered in Bernardo's clean visage.

I had seen Bernardo for the first time on television at the orphanage, the day after the murder, the 17th of May 1975. On the screen, Bernardo was holding his mother's hand while the reporter interviewed Martin Esteban. The family stood in front of a church.

"It's a tragedy," Esteban said in response to the reporter's question, "a personal one and one for the world of business. Señor Fuertes was a formidable captain of industry." Esteban's expression captured the right attitude of personal pain restrained by the solemnity and control of a professional. His white shirt gleamed against his suit—the lie of that bright crispness had almost, almost, unleashed the violent hatred charging through me as I watched with the other children. But I stayed quiet.

"You say *personal*?" the intense-looking reporter had prompted, exaggerated curiosity in his voice.

"He was my business partner, of course. We operated

factories in Bilbao. But he was also a friend of many years."

In the background, people streamed to the building, darting glances at the camera. Señora Esteban, a striking woman with dark almond-shaped eyes, seemed uncomfortable as she tugged on the lace mantilla tied beneath her chin. Next to her, beautiful Bernardo, in short pants and starched collar, was serene.

The reporter had pressed on. "Señor Fuertes must have had enemies?"

Esteban had shrugged. "What industrialist does not? Disgruntled workers come with the territory. Competitors too."

"A competitor is capable of this?"

"*Porque no?*" Esteban came off as cool, uninterested in elaborating on the obvious.

"You are a friend of Generalissimo Franco. What reaction has the President to this murder?"

"I can't speak for the President. Naturally the tragedy must grieve him." The church bell tolled. "I'm sorry, mass is beginning." Esteban had nodded politely and ushered his wife and son forward.

The son. No plan about the son had sprung into my mind in that moment. No plan to use Bernardo to get to Esteban. But the boy had left an indelible impression, like grace or original sin or whatever the hell mark the human soul carried, according to the good sisters at the orphanage. Before any plan came to be, there was that beautiful, wistful face of the son, who would clearly never shake his fist in the face of God as his father did.

It was that innocent face that had captivated me. At first it was the focus of all my hatred, and the innocence I vowed to ravage the way my own innocence had been ravaged. I had conjured it in my mind when Maria Rosario beat me and in my own cruelest moments—when I was slicing the arms of playmates with the pocket knife I eventually used to cut up my own arms.

Like the spirit of God in Genesis, the face of Bernardo brooded over the chaos until the kind priests took me from the nuns and I stopped lashing out aimlessly, futilely. Then, when I learned that Bernardo had entered the Salesian seminary, that face served a new, creative purpose. A plan inspired by the face, my own creation story, took form—the water of it, the dry land, the seas, the sun, and the moon.

I re-created myself as model student, soccer captain, devout Catholic, and finally, priest. My position was strategic, within monastic walls where I could work with impunity. What's more, from my first glimpse of the grown Bernardo, I felt more sure of what I'd suspected from the moment I saw him on the TV screen. He was a boy who could be taken the way I'd imagined taking the waiter.

Four
BERNARDO

Abbot Baroja introduced Juan Ramón to us in the dining hall on his first morning.

"Padre Juan Ramón comes to us from El Sacro Corazón," Baroja said.

He and Juan Ramón stood between the two long tables that stood side by side. All 20 of us monks looked up, nodding and smiling.

"I'm very grateful for the generosity of the community at Salamanca," the abbot continued. "And I have to say, it's a pleasure to have some young blood among us wizened relics."

Everybody laughed. They were all over 50, several in their 80s. I was the only young monk. And now Juan Ramón. He looked at me. My face burned, but I didn't lower my eyes.

"A heart-felt welcome to you, Juan Ramón," Baroja said.

When he reached out and patted Juan Ramón's back, I detected the new monk's annoyance, quickly transformed into a forced smile.

That distaste for easy affection, even more than the toreador's face, stirred me. I finally dropped my gaze to the empty bowl at my place. *No risks, no risks*, I told myself. My heart was beating like the pump in the monastery's crypt after the water pipes had burst the winter before, releasing an icy flood into the mausoleum of Santo Domingo's first abbot. A plaque engraved in Latin had loosened and floated down to the boiler room.

When the abbot finished introducing Juan Ramón, he made the daily announcements.

Avoiding Juan Ramón's glance, I listened attentively. I was grateful to Father Baroja. He'd given me a fatherly welcome when I arrived after novitiate and had found me the perfect teaching assignment at San Servando Boy's Home.

And the most important thing: Despite all my fears, he was ready to approve me for ordination on the Feast of Pentecost, only a year away. He'd sent for the papers to be stamped and filed with the father superior in Madrid. Nothing short of a debauched lapse into an episode like the scene at Figueroa could make me lose my place before the bishop.

After breakfast I waited my turn to welcome Juan Ramón. I had no choice. My throat was tight and dry by the time he came to me. I looked directly at him. What else could I do?

"Ah, Brother Bernardo," he said when I introduced myself. "*Congratulaciones!* Abbot González announced that you took your final vows last month."

"Yes, thanks."

He was slightly taller than me. His black scapular fell from broad shoulders. Fleshy pectoral muscles filled out his habit. His body was trim and, I suspected, firm. He had the intense, disciplined look of a bullfighter who had captivated me when I was a teenager—Miguel Lopez, a beautiful, strapping man who after all his narrow escapes in the ring was killed in an automobile accident outside of Cádiz. Juan Ramón was not as perfectly handsome as Lopez had been. His aquiline nose was prominent. One eyebrow had a gap, as though scar tissue from some wound kept hair from growing there. But his olive skin was clear, and dark stubble accentuated a powerful jaw and beautifully sculpted throat. A goatee framed his full lips.

"Where are you stationed?" he said. His eyes, brown as Moroccan leather, were so fierce and sad they could have been painted by Goya and El Greco working as a team.

"At San Servando Home for Boys."

"Oh? What do you do there?"

"I teach history," I said. "And help supervise." I lowered my eyes, unable to bear his direct gaze.

"When do classes start?"

"At 10."

He looked at his watch. "You've got two hours. Would you mind showing me the way to Santiago del

Arrabal? It's my assignment. Maybe you could give me a little tour of Toledo along the way. Consider it a work of mercy."

I smiled.

"That means yes, right?"

"Let me get my things," I said. "I'll meet you in the entrance hall."

I raced down the corridor and up the staircase near the porter's office to my cell on the second floor at the end of the dark hallway, near the head of the chapel. *Where is Juan Ramón's*, I wondered? *Has Baroja arranged for the two young monks to lodge near each other?*

Adrenaline shot through me at the thought. For the past six months since final vows I'd been lonely for someone my own age. And now this dark newcomer. *Just for me*, I thought. Then I tried to reign in the rushing feelings and think of my Beloved.

I grabbed my backpack from my desk and was starting out the door when I went to the saucer-sized mirror above the sink. My face was flushed from running. The color was becoming. And I no longer looked like a skinny teenager. My face had filled out. It was heart-shaped, a cleft in my chin. My eyes were quiet but determined, green as a cat's, and the strabismus wasn't bad.

That was the real reason I had gone to the mirror, to see how bad the strange cast seemed. Sometimes in photographs my eyes looked nearly crossed. I liked to imagine that the pictures were taken before I was ready, before I could concentrate and keep my gaze perfect.

Of course, the strabismus hadn't mattered that day in a dark backroom of Figueroa...

...

I'll never forget that first morning with Juan Ramón, touring the cathedral, standing at Bisagra Gate. He could see through my defenses from the beginning. That ability was my downfall. He won me over so easily, so smoothly. At Bisagra he leaned against the stone wall of the Moorish gate and crossed his arms. His sleeves rode up, exposing his meaty forearms.

"Coming to a new community isn't easy," I said, awkward in a silent moment after my rambling about buildings and statues.

"I'll tell you the truth, Bernardo. It takes me a long time to adjust to new people. I'm not one to make friends easily. I've always been a loner." His chocolate eyes inspected me with boldness.

"So have I." I removed my backpack from my shoulder, set it on the ground, and slipped my hands into my pockets.

"Do you like it at Santo Domingo? Among all the old relics—wasn't that the abbot's word? When he introduced me to everyone."

I shrugged. "I'm glad they're all so much older than I am, so comfortable in monastic life. They make it seem easy."

"You don't find life in the cloister easy?"

"Oh, the cloister is fine. I love the quiet and the order. I only mean that...well, let's just say I'm barely a toddler in the way of perfection."

He extended his hand. "Congratulations. Now you have company."

He clasped my hand for a long moment. That's the first time *he* made me feel the burning band through my crotch, like a saddle blazing and vibrating at the same time. All day I thought about him and that night in my hot bed I couldn't get him out of my thoughts.

I would have given in to the fantasies, I would have touched myself if the naked Cristo hadn't saved me.

•••

When Juan Ramón found out that I jogged early every morning, he joined me. Over the next couple of weeks, we ran side by side through the streets of Toledo while the city still slept. It excited me to run next to him, listening to him breathe, racing him for long stretches, laughing when he teased me. I spent a good part of the recreation period with him too. *No danger*, I thought. *He isn't the one with the attractions, and I can resist mine. I have to.*

One Saturday morning Juan Ramón led the way through Bisagra Gate and we jogged along the city wall in the direction of the train station, uphill all the way. It was just after dawn. The air was sharp and clean. Faint clouds wisped across the sky. Juan Ramón wore a purple T-shirt and gray jogging shorts.

We'd jogged through shaded alleys to the gate. The sun struck us all at once, like a spotlight. It felt good running next to him. He signaled directions as though he'd run the route a thousand times, with me at his side. Technically we were breaking the Grand Silence, but Juan Ramón had brushed off my scrupulosity. When else could we run to minimize the summer heat? The Sabbath was made for man, he'd reminded me, grinning, not man for the Sabbath.

"What's that?" he said.

I saw something small and dark scamper across the road. "A rabbit?"

"No. Wait a minute." He dug through a clump of wild grass growing along the wall and pulled out a scrawny black kitten. He held it against his sweat-darkened T-shirt and scratched it behind the ears. "The mother must be around somewhere."

He held out the kitten for me to pet.

"Look how big the ears are," I said.

Juan Ramón nodded. "I can see why you thought it was a rabbit."

We hadn't walked 10 meters before a lanky black cat with a white spot above her eye sauntered out onto the road. She faced us and complained. We found a litter of kittens licking each other near a crate turned on its side.

"She must have had them in there." Juan Ramón gently placed the kitten next to a sibling who swiped at it playfully. The mother came over to inspect the returned baby. "Let's take them back with us."

"Baroja wouldn't like it," I said.

"Why not? We could keep them in the courtyard."

"We'd have to feed the mother. She wouldn't be able to forage in the city."

"Then I'll take them to Santiago." Juan Ramón started collecting the kittens in the crate.

When I tried to pick up the mother, she hissed, clawed my hand, and darted up the road.

Juan Ramón set the crate down and examined my hand. A thread of blood oozed across the palm. "Not too bad." He raised my hand to his face, almost as though he planned to kiss it.

"It's all right."

"We could get it bandaged at Santiago. We're not far."

"It's fine," I said, touched by his concern.

We forgot about the cats and jogged to the river and then along the embankment back toward the monastery. We made it back in time to shower before morning prayers. But I hadn't cooled down from the run and my habit clung to my back. Across the aisle from me, Juan Ramón followed the psalms, strands of wet black hair plastered to his temples and forehead.

• • •

Some evenings we would sit in the warm courtyard and discuss whatever came to mind—the boys at San Servando, where I taught, Juan Ramón's parish, monks we both knew. Sometimes, Juan Ramón talked about his childhood.

"The nuns at the orphanage were like Nazis," he said one evening as we strolled around the rose garden in the courtyard. "They got off on torturing us. One nun especially—Maria Rosario. She used to beat my bare ass. Gave her a thrill."

Brother Vicente cast Juan Ramón a look of disapproval from the other side of the garden. He was the obese monk who lumbered up and down the corridors ringing a bell to wake us for morning prayers. Juan Ramón waved to him and chuckled when Vicente reached down to inspect a rose as though he hadn't seen him.

"The mother superior let her get away with it?" I said.

"Don't stir the waters. That was her policy. She backed her girls one hundred percent. Of course, I doubt she knew the kinds of things Maria Rosario said. She liked to taunt me about my parents. Said they deserved to die."

"My God."

Juan Ramón nodded. "I'm not making it up. She was a damned monster."

I wanted him to tell me more about his parents, but the bell for compline tolled. I decided I should wait for him to bring up the subject again.

A few days later he did. He told me how they died. It was a Sunday afternoon, when we monks were free to wander through Toledo or visit our families if they lived nearby. Juan Ramón and I strolled through a labyrinth of shaded streets and bright plazas bustling with tourists and locals. The scent of cilantro and peppers and onions wafted from restaurants and kitchen windows.

Juan Ramón recognized the avenue leading to Santiago del Arrabal. We walked along the wide road for a few minutes until we came to the Mosque of Bab Al Mardu. I'd pointed it out during our first walk through the city. Naturally the mosque had been renamed by the Church; Cristo de la Luz was its Christian name. We passed through a doorless archway into the shade of the small building. I walked under a series of keyhole-shaped arches to some stone steps in the front of the square room. Juan Ramón stayed back near the entrance. He leaned against the wall and took in the whole space.

"So, you like this place?" he said.

I nodded. "It's had quite a history. First a Visigoth church, then a mosque, then reconsecrated by the Church. The Church Triumphant."

"Funny." Juan Ramón was examining the arches rising

from the columns. "I'm inspired by its pagan roots. I read somewhere that human sacrifices occurred under these very stones."

He seemed to be in a dark mood. I wanted him to open up, but I was afraid to push him. "Where you're standing is the original Visigoth church," I said.

"The Visigoths. Now there was a group with some balls, *que no*? No pussyfooting around with civilized laws. Just draw and quarter whoever they wanted to—on the spot." He spit across the stone floor and glanced up at me, his nostrils flaring.

I stared at him, puzzled.

"My parents were murdered, Bernardo."

"Murdered?"

"Yes, murdered. Killed. Executed."

"At home?"

Juan Ramón nodded. "For money."

"The killer...did they get him?"

"Madrid's fine police turned a blind eye."

"So he's still out there?"

"Apparently."

A woman's laughter suddenly echoed through the building. A beautiful girl with long dark hair darted through the entrance, chased by a stocky boy in a red T-shirt. When the girl saw me, she stopped and put her hand to her mouth, obviously embarrassed.

"*Lo siento*, Padre!" she apologized. "Stop it, Miguel." She turned and pulled her hand away from the boy, who was tugging on it, apparently unconcerned that a monk was observing his romantic antics. Then her bright eyes fell on Juan Ramón. She gazed at him with interest.

Juan Ramón unabashedly returned her gaze. She was a voluptuous girl, in blue jeans and a form fitting knit top. Her lips were full and her olive complexion clear and lustrous.

"*Buenos Días*," he said.

"*Buenos Días*, Padre," she mumbled back, nodding respectfully. Then she advanced to the door, signaling for the boy to follow her.

"Beautiful!" Juan Ramón said when the pair had gone.

I nodded perfunctorily.

"What! Don't tell me you think a monk shouldn't notice something like that?" Juan Ramón gestured toward the entrance. "I may be celibate but I'm not dead." He came over and sat down next to me on the stone steps. "The girl reminds me of a woman at the parish I was assigned to in Salamanca before my ordination. She came to me for counseling. Her marriage was falling apart, she said. She was stunning. The kind of woman you can't keep your eyes off. Long legs, sexy smile." He seemed to watch me for my response. "Anyway, you know the type."

I looked away.

"Don't tell me you've never been laid?" Juan Ramón shook me by the arm. "Well, I told myself I wouldn't enter the monastery unless I knew what I was giving up. Believe me, when I took my vows I felt the sacrifice in my bones. I still do...when I go without." He studied me. "Some of us don't have your virtue."

"I'm no saint," I said. My nipples and groin buzzed and my stomach was quivering. Juan Ramón smelled musky from the walk. He'd hiked up his habit over his knees. His calves bulged with muscles the size of mangoes. His athletic, finely sculptured feet looked like a gladiator's in their black sandals.

"No?"

"Don't you think I have my own demons? We all do."

Juan Ramón grinned. His goatee made him look devilish. "I don't believe it. You're the perfect monk from what I can see."

I took a deep breath to calm myself. I got up and walked to the closest of three side doorways and peered out. "The passion you talk about—of course I understand it. And that's why I became a monk." I turned to him. "Have you read San Juan de la Cruz's 'Spiritual Canticle'?"

"Can't say that I have," Juan Ramón replied, yawning.

" 'Extinguish these miseries,' he says, 'Reveal Your presence oh spring like crystal, Withdraw them, Beloved.' "

"And so Christ is your beloved?"

"Yes, Christ."

"And the miseries you want to extinguish?"

I shrugged. "Separation, any separation from Christ. I want perfect communion. San Juan had mystical experiences."

"I hear mystical experiences are hard to come by."

"I'd settle for crumbs."

Juan Ramón got up and came over to me. He clasped me by the arm and pressed his lips to my ear. His goatee scratched the skin.

My heart pounded.

"You don't have to settle for anything," he whispered.

Five

JUAN RAMÓN

I had no problem adapting to the rhythm of daily life at Santo Domingo. The routines from monastery to monastery varied little. Matins, chanted at the crack of dawn, started the day. Then after breakfast came the duties assigned to each monk individually by the abbot.

I learned that, along with Bernardo, five of Santo Domingo's monks worked at the San Servando Home for Boys. They assisted a small group of Salesians who actually lived on the premises rather than in the monastery. Several of Santo Domingo's other monks took care of operations in the monastery itself: the porter, the cook, the librarian, and those who cleaned and maintained the buildings. The rest had duties in Toledo parishes. Apparently there was a scarcity of diocesan priests in the city, as there was in most cities in Spain. But religious communities still had a ready supply of priests and were regularly called upon for their services.

Before dinner the monks assembled in the chapel for vespers. The evening meal was always eaten in silence while someone read from the lives of the saints or another equally dull spiritual treatise. After dinner we moved down to the recreation hall on the ground floor for an hour of socializing. Afterward we were free to use the library or the exercise room or to stroll in the courtyard until 9 o'clock, when the bell for compline rang and we headed back to the chapel. After compline we retired to our cells and the Grand Silence began, not to be lifted until breakfast the next morning.

I'd observed such a schedule for the past eight years of my life, since completing a bachelor's degree at the university in Salamanca. As a novice I'd studied theology as well as the Salesian constitutions, and endured lectures about the order and about contemplative spirituality. After the two-year novitiate, I took temporary vows and taught religion at a high school in Salamanca. After four years of proving myself as teacher and monk, I made my final profession. Ordination came only after another two years of teaching and parish work.

The decision to join the order had been purely practical: Even a spy could not ask for a better cover, nor for a base more secure and undemanding of his labor or energy. But I'd come to appreciate the company of the brothers. Many were ready to chat when I felt like it, and most were happy to leave me alone when I didn't. As for the religious dimension of the life, I had no objection to it. Doctrines meant nothing to me, but the chants were soothing and the rituals familiar. I admired the faith of the monks and shared their belief in a God who created and ordered the universe. But I'd be damned if I would ever worship their God of unconditional forgiveness. Mine was the Old Testament's God of justice—the God who exposed the lascivious elders of Babylon plotting the ruin of Susannah, the God who fortified young David against a giant Philistine. The theology professors had dismissed this avenging God. According to them, Susannah received no personal satisfaction for exposing the elders, and David fought for Israel, not himself. I knew better. Susannah and David were flesh and blood. They prized their own worth and asserted it even to the point of bloodshed. What God brought out of their revenge for Israel or anyone else was not their concern. Who knows the mind of God? Man's business is to know his own mind, and he sins when he ignores its commands.

As for celibacy, I didn't know the meaning of the word. I had known I was a *maricon* the first time I saw a broad-chested maintenance man with his shirt off at San Salvador's—I must have been 9 or 10. But I didn't try to fuck a boy until I was 14. One Saturday the brothers at the Salesian home were treating us to a movie in the auditorium. I sat next to a new kid who had been making me hot. He was a pretty boy about my age, with dark, curly lashes and a pig tail. His slight lisp had already brought him some taunts. In the locker room I'd noticed his round ass. I'd jerked off with boys before but I'd never had an ass and I imagined taking his. I'd sat next to him several times in the dining hall and he'd let me grope his crotch under the table.

I whispered in his ear and he followed me out of the dark auditorium like a lamb. We climbed up to the dormitory, forbidden ground during the day—the brothers were smart. I rammed my tongue into his mouth, instinctively, like a bird feeding her baby, and he greedily sucked it. Unzipping my jeans, I forced him to his knees and made him take me. He gagged a couple of times, but his head soon moved rhythmically and I had to make him stop before I exploded. I pulled him to his feet and unfastened his pants. I pushed him face down onto my bed. I was too green to realize you needed some kind of lubrication. But I wanted him and I struggled for quite a while before I gave up and shot my load on his two smooth mounds. While I was jerking him off I got so hot I did myself again.

What I didn't get there, I got the next week, when I was farmed out to a rich couple who had a whim to share some weekends with an underprivileged boy. They gave me the key to their apartment so I could let myself in after school. I had the place to myself for an hour or so before they got home from work. I got permission for Luis—Luis Navarro was his name—to come over one night. The building was a new high-rise near Puerto del Sol. We took the elevator to the seventh floor. We crossed through the large living room filled with white leather furniture on our way to my room. His hair was untied now and moved like silk as he walked. An aquarium gurgled away in my room, a half dozen tropical fish darting through the quivering plants. He stuck his hand in the tank and wiped the water on my face. "Cool down, hot boy," he said. I pushed him down onto the bed and stripped off his jeans and T-shirt. I lubed up with lotion from the woman's bathroom. Sinking deep into his warmth and tightness, I thought I'd died and gone to heaven.

After Luis, whenever I couldn't take another minute inside the walls of San Juan Bosco, when my youthful hormones were making me crazy with heat, I found my way to some bars I'd heard about in Figueroa. Later, when I officially entered the Salesian community, it actually became easier to get away. I had to run errands for the community, and I had to take the subway to the school where I taught. And there were boys to be had even within the holy community. A few times I took advantage of them. By and large, though, I didn't risk it. I knew that getting caught could ruin everything for me.

Six

BERNARDO

As much as I wanted to hear more about Juan Ramón's parents, I didn't bring up the subject again. The hateful look in his eyes as he talked about their murder got to me. He almost seemed to blame me. He scared me. Besides, I figured he would talk about it when he was ready.

At the end of June the monastery had its annual open-house.

All the monks invited their families for Sunday mass and dinner. My mother was coming. My father wasn't, naturally. He'd cut me out of his life the day I announced my plans to join the Salesians. That was on a morning just after my 14th birthday.

"Please tell me I didn't hear right!" he'd said, looking up from his morning paper. Maria, an old servant, had just placed his coffee before him and he waved her away when she asked if he wanted anything special from the cook.

"It's something I've prayed about for a long time, Father." I glanced at my mother for support. I'd long ago opened my heart to her. She looked up from her cup, her eyes full of empathy, but helplessness. "God is calling me," I said.

My father snorted. His dark, hard face had just been shaved by his valet and it gleamed with lotion. "God does not call an Esteban to priesthood. We're industrialists. We're the life of Spain. We saved it from collapse under the communists. We saved the Church too. Never forget that. If you want to serve God, make Spain a formidable power in Europe, instead of taking the woman's way out." He glanced hatefully at Mama, who was on the verge of tears.

"You don't care about Spain," I blurted, despite my resolution to ignore his insults. "You care only about yourself. Your position. Your money. You'd sell Spain out in a minute if it meant more for you."

My father laughed. "This is excellent. The pious little runt thinks he can shame his father." He addressed these words to an imaginary audience. Then he turned to me. "Something went wrong with you, Bernardo. Maybe I slapped you one time too many. Or maybe I didn't slap you enough."

"Stop it, Martin!" Mama slammed down her cup. She was beautiful still at 40, her face translucent and smooth, her dark, luscious hair swept back into a French roll. "You're ruining everything for him. Let him have his day, for God's sake."

"*You've* ruined everything for him," my father shouted. "I wanted to make a man out of him."

I stood and threw my napkin on the table. "I can't wait to get out of this house."

"You're a little hypocrite," Father called after me as I left the dining room, "too much of a coward to face the real world."

I stopped and turned around. "The world of Martin Esteban?" I spoke to the back of his head since he wouldn't deign to look at me. "You're right, it scares me. Thank God."

I did my best to wipe Martin Esteban out of my mind. If it hadn't been for my mother, who put up with the back of his hand and even his fist, I might have been successful. Whenever she showed up at the monastery with a bruised face, I could taste my hatred. My father was right, I was a hypocrite. I hated him too much to forgive him and feared him too much to confront him about Mama.

The day before the open house, Baroja assigned us all tasks to prepare the monastery. Before starting ours, Juan Ramón suggested we say a rosary together. He'd noticed I usually said mine after breakfast. We knelt side by side at the communion rail. The citrus scent of his shampoo was clean and strong.

"Let's say it in Latin," he said. He crossed himself with the silver crucifix of his rosary and then kissed it. He nodded to me. "You lead."

I forged through the creed without a single mistake. I wanted Juan Ramón to admire my mastery of Latin. The simple *paters* and *aves* rolled off my tongue. When I finished the first decade, he announced the second mystery, the Ascension.

"Jesus rockets to heaven," he said.

I laughed.

With the first *ave*, all traces of irreverence left his voice. He knelt straight as a military guard, his eyes fixed on the tabernacle. "*Ave Maria, gratia plena, Dominus tecum.*" The pronunciation was deliberate, solemn. He spoke with authority, as though his job, like Gabriel's, was to convince the Virgin of her favor with God.

"Good Latin, Bernardo," he said as we left the chapel. He reached into the holy water font by the door and extended his wet fingertips to me. We both made the sign of the cross.

A pickup truck delivered fruit at the side entrance of the monastery. Juan Ramón and I had been assigned to lug the heavy crates into the kitchen. We each took an end and descended the long flight of stairs, Juan Ramón positioned at the bottom, his back to me. Brother Arturo, the husky cook in his mid 50s, relieved me once, but Juan Ramón wouldn't take a break. However, after we'd carried in four crates, he did let me lead the way down the stairs. I had to take one step at a time.

"Easy does it, Bernardo," Brother Arturo said. He was at the bottom of the stairs, holding the door open. "We're not in any rush."

"Don't worry, I'm fine." Sweat streamed down my face. A few stairs from the bottom, I slipped and dropped my end of the crate. An avalanche of oranges rolled down the steps. I stopped in my tracks, my face burning from embarrassment.

Brother Arturo clapped his hands to his face and shook his head. "Santa Maria. They'll be bruised."

Juan Ramón laughed. He picked up an orange and tossed it at my head. I didn't duck in time, and it thudded on my crown. "That's all right, Arturo. Bernardo will go out and pick some more."

As the three of us gathered the oranges, Juan Ramón rubbed the top of my head. "No permanent damage, is there?"

I smiled. "Just to my pride."

That afternoon Juan Ramón and I set up tables in the courtyard and mopped the corridors on the main floors. After the mishap on the stairs, our movements were perfectly coordinated. We seemed to communicate without words. He would nod his head in one direction and I would have my end of the table in position instantly or the bucket rolled to him before he could ask. The chores were the kind I usually hated, but with Juan Ramón they were easy. The hours passed quickly and quietly.

That night during the recreation hour, Arturo gathered Diego, Baroja, and several other monks around us and recounted my spill on the steps. Juan Ramón laughed so hard, he had to wipe the tears from his eyes. When he patted my back, I loosened up and laughed too.

At noon the next day I was in place with the other monks in the choir stalls. The room was packed for mass. Some of the monks had huge extended families and the pews were filled with widowed sisters, grown nieces and nephews, their children, and even their grandchildren. The normally quiet, solemn space reverberated with the sound of babies crying and kneelers dropping and coughing and sneezing and subdued chatter. Brother Eduardo did his best to cover it up with the organ prelude, which got louder and louder.

I glanced over at my mother. She was in a front pew, saying a rosary. A black lace mantilla framed her face. Her eyes were fixed on the saint-filled niches of the high altar. As usual she seemed sad. I wished she didn't have to go back to him. If my assignment after ordination took me to Salamanca or Seville, where would she go to escape?

Juan Ramón was the principle celebrant for mass. Flanked at the altar by Baroja and the five ordained brothers at Santo Domingo, he was like a perfect, strong-stalked lily in a row of withered blossoms. His oiled hair and his goatee were raven against his white chasuble. His full lips moved with sensual determination as he read the Eucharistic prayer. When he genuflected at the consecration, he did it with perfect agility, without using the altar for support.

In the corridor after mass, I introduced him to my mother.

"*Mucho gusto*, Señora." He clasped her hand when she offered it to him. He stared at her, as though he'd seen her before.

She wore an indigo linen dress with a jacket. She looked uncomfortable. She had removed her mantilla and now nervously smoothed her hair. "Bernardo tells me you're new at Santo Domingo, Father. How do you like Toledo?"

"Very well, Señora. I'm getting to know it. Bernardo's been showing me around. Are you here alone?"

"Yes. My driver brought me."

"Father doesn't come to these things," I said to rescue her.

"*Que lastima!*" Juan Ramón said. "Brother Alfonso's cooked up quite a treat, I hear. *Huevos a caballo*. Do you like partridge, Señora? I hear it's a specialty of Toledo."

She nodded. "*Claro*, Father."

"*Bueno*," he said. "Maybe we should make our way to the dining hall."

Juan Ramón offered her his arm and she took it out of politeness, I thought. In the dining hall Juan Ramón and I sat on either side of her. Across from us were Brother Jaime, the silver-haired librarian, and the rotund Brother Vicente, both nonstop talkers. They took up most of my mother's attention. Juan Ramón was especially quiet. He seemed mesmerized by her. Several times during the meal I looked over and caught him staring at her.

Before she left, Mama invited Juan Ramón to dinner the following Sunday, my grandmother's birthday.

"I would be delighted, Señora."

I threw her a glance that said, *What are you doing?* When I told her goodbye at the car, I asked her about it.

"It's my house too, Bernardo." She kissed me and climbed into the back seat of the blue sedan.

That afternoon Juan Ramón and I walked to the Synagogue of the Transito in the old Jewish quarter. It was 4 o'clock and the bright sun beat fiercely on the pale bricks of the 14th-century building. Its Moorish windows reminded me of hooded snakes. Juan Ramón asked me about my childhood in Madrid, and I described my privileged life—the mansion, servants, lessons in tennis and horseback riding.

"How could you leave all that?" Juan Ramón said. We were sitting on the ground under the shade of a cypress. He leaned back against the tree.

I shrugged. "Priesthood. It's all I ever wanted. I couldn't wait to get to the seminary."

"Sounds like you were relieved to get out of the house."

"I was," I admitted.

"Your father?"

I nodded.

"Even some of the greatest saints didn't get along with their fathers. Look at San Francisco de Assisi."

"Oh, San Francisco."

"What's the matter? San Francisco is not saint enough for you?"

"He just came from a different world." I pulled a blade of grass and examined it.

Juan Ramón waited.

"All right. If you want to know the truth, my father, Martin Esteban, has never concerned himself with anything but earthly treasures—in his case, profits from his business. He heads a very formidable manufacturing company."

"In Madrid?" Juan Ramón said.

"Bilbao. The business has claimed all his time—and his love. Basically, he's an idolater and an adulterer—since his business has always taken my mother's place. And if there were a commandment against neglecting your children, he would definitely be guilty of that too."

"But he did provide for you."

"Oh, yes, magnificently. I've already told you, we lived in a palace near the Jardines del Retiro in Madrid. We had our own lake and gardens and tennis court and pool. Servants woke us in the morning, brought us our towels, our tea, my father's cocktails—when he indulged us with his presence."

"Does he still live in this mansion?" Juan Ramón asked.

I tossed the blade of grass away and stretched out on the ground, my hands behind my head. "He's never *lived* there. But, yes, he resides on the premises, mostly in his own apartments."

"Apartments? This sounds like the Palacio Real."

I nodded. "One wing of the house contains his office,

his bedroom and sitting room, his weight room and sauna, and even a pool. My mother and I are forbidden to enter that wing."

"His bedroom? So, your mother and father..."

"No," I quickly interrupted, "they don't sleep together. I can't remember my parents ever sharing the same room."

When I look back now, Juan Ramón's interest in my parents didn't seem odd. He just wanted to know me, my history, and they were part of it. And he was challenging me to face the facts of my life. Now, of course, I see his curiosity in a completely different light.

"You know, Bernardo," he said, stretching out next to me. "Our spiritual development can't be separated from our childhood development."

"I didn't know you were a psychologist," I said.

"But it makes sense, doesn't it?" Juan Ramón rolled over onto his elbow. His face was just above mine. I could see the stubble on his throat. "We base our image of God on our father, right? If we haven't made peace with the earthly father, our concept of God is flawed. We turn Him into either a demon or a fairy-tale character."

"A fairy-tale character?"

"Naturally. He becomes an unreal fairy godfather—everything our father was not. Now *there's* an idol for you."

"But God *is* perfect!"

"Perfect? You mean static and sterile? Some grinning cartoon character watching over us from a cloud?" Juan Ramón shook his head. "The real God has sweat on his brow and blood on his hands. Just like us. And if you turn him into an inept clown, you just might end up staring at your creation for a boring eternity."

I took in his words. Everything from his mouth sounded right. His strength made me want him to lead me the way the stranger in Figueroa had led me—to a dark, sweet encounter.

When I look back, I see straight through my self-deception. I think from the moment Juan Ramón's lips brushed my ear that afternoon at Cristo de la Luz, I recognized his desires—and their direction. The girl who'd come running into the Mosque was not the one who caught his eye. It was the stocky boy in the red T-shirt. His black trousers had bulged at the crotch—I had noticed that, and the bulge traveled down his leg a piece. He was hard for the girl. But I was hard for him. So was Juan Ramón, I'd suspected. When his bearded chin tickled my ear, I was excited and triumphant. He wanted me too. But I resisted seeing the truth as long as I could.

Seven

Juan Ramón

Bernardo's hair was cropped close, the hairline from ear to neck to ear clean. Angelic and pure. I sat three meters behind him in the presider's chair, sweltering in chasuble on top of habit. At least my damned feet were cool in their sandals. He sang in Latin since it was Sunday mass. "*Cantate Domino, omnes gentes.*" Sing to the Lord, all you people. His voice rose like a tenor flute. No vibrato, no power, but true. Sincere. Like Bernardo himself. Don't think I was so hard or cynical that I didn't believe in sincerity, misguided or not.

"Excellent sermon, Father," said Brother Eduardo. He

was a narrow-eyed, petty little monk who dispensed compliments as if they were rubies. No, *a* ruby, spit out of his pursed lips at the lucky beneficiary.

I nodded my thanks all the same. Baroja, Jaime, and Pedro, the other concelebrants, had already left the sacristy. Bernardo was at the sink, dumping the basin used for washing the celebrant's hands before the consecration.

"Wasn't Father's sermon excellent?" Eduardo said to Bernardo.

"Very original." Bernardo looked over his shoulder at me. "I don't think I've ever heard a sermon on Jesus driving the money lenders out of the temple."

"It's good to be reminded of God's anger," Eduardo said. "Too much milky compassion nowadays."

Bernardo nodded politely. I went to the sink, took the basin from him, and dried it. I handed him the cruet of water to dump and poured the wine from the other cruet back into the bottle.

Eduardo clicked his tongue. "That's not good, Father. Bernardo's the acolyte. Let him tend the vessels."

"Should he wipe my ass too?" I asked. I winked at Bernardo.

The color spread across Eduardo's little round face. He bowed to the crucifix above the wardrobe and pranced out of the sacristy.

"Not a good way to make friends," Bernardo said.

"Not a friend I care to make."

We finished cleaning up and walked to the café in the plaza across from the monastery. It was mid afternoon. Sunday mass at Santo Domingo was late to accommodate the monks who said morning mass in their parishes. It was hot and the four outside tables were empty, even though umbrellas shaded them. The tables inside were crowded. Chatter and laughter poured out the open doors.

"Let's sit out here," I said.

Bernardo nodded and an oily-haired waiter seated us and took our orders.

"So, you didn't like my sermon?"

Bernardo shrugged. "It's not how I see God. At least not how I want to see him."

"Vindictive, you mean?"

"Waiting for us to choose the wrong door, where a tiger is waiting."

I laughed. "I didn't say that. I said he gets angry and that makes him real, like a human."

"Now *that* I believe."

"Is that why you entered the order?" I was genuinely curious. How did the son of Esteban end up this way?

Bernardo gazed across the plaza at the facade of Santo Domingo's chapel. The two towers were washed in bright sunlight.

Bernardo's clear skin seemed almost translucent. His cat eyes were big and soft. He wouldn't be so bad in bed, I imagined. I would willingly break in his sweet, tight ass.

"When I was little I went to daily mass with my mother," he said. "I couldn't understand much, but I looked at the pictures in her prayer book. Jesus with the children. Jesus healing the blind man. Jesus talking to Martha and Mary. And it clicked for me. Jesus up there in the host, everyone kneeling to him; it was the same Jesus I saw in the pictures. He loved me. No matter what. No matter who didn't."

"You mean your father."

Bernardo stared at the monastery without speaking. His eyes filled. "I wanted to give myself to Christ. When I made my first communion I was so excited I threw up."

The waiter brought us our coffees. We drank them in a few gulps. "Love doesn't preclude anger, Bernardo. Just the opposite."

He looked at me.

"God is damned angry about cruelty," I said. "I think he's angry about little people like Eduardo and their power games."

"My father never beat me."

"That makes him a saint?"

Bernardo's eyes fell to his cup. "It's not about him, anyway. I've loved God for as long as I can remember. I loved watching the candles flicker in church, and the chants, and the pictures and statues. They were all about God. God was everywhere, my mother told me. Deep in my heart. With me. For me."

"Except when you hate. Is that what you think?"

"Yes." He raised his eyes. An eagerness filled them, hope for something that eluded his convictions. This was good.

"Even then," I assured him.

• • •

The day I went with Bernardo to Madrid was sweltering. The stones and bricks of Toledo's Zocodover Plaza radiated the heat as though they were coals.

It was a Sunday, and the usual crowds of tourists at the outdoor cafés there gathered under the shade of yellow umbrellas. A few heads turned as Bernardo and I stepped out into the bright square from the cool, narrow Calle Comercio. The customers probably enjoyed the quaint sight of two monks in long robes and sandals, imagining the holy brothers relished their secure life, away from the corrupt world. If they only knew.

We passed the Hospital de Santa Cruz, the intricate bas reliefs of its facade aglow in the blazing sun, and descended the stone steps of Calle Miguel de Cervantes to the Alcántara Bridge. In the heat, even the muddy river below seemed inviting. By the time we arrived at the train station, a 15-minute walk, we were both sopping with sweat. We washed our faces in the rest room and sat on benches inside the station to cool down. Within 20 minutes the train to Madrid pulled up to the platform.

The air-conditioned car of the train felt like heaven compared to the hot monastery, which had never been fitted with a modern cooling system.

Despite Bernardo's restless fidgeting, I closed my eyes and tried to relax as the train sped along the open countryside between Toledo and Madrid. But I was too wound up to rest. That very day I would come face to face with the animal that murdered my parents. Just seeing Esteban's wife had made my heart beat like a time bomb. I would now enter Esteban's own home as a guest and size up the man over a glass of his own wine. Esteban's arrogant face would rally and focus the hatred that had festered and hardened in me for all these years—until it had become a kind of ugly grinning charm that I dared pull from its hiding place only infrequently and briefly if I wanted to stay sane. Now, as I drew near to taking his life, I could transform that hideous object into a dynamic part of my chemistry, like blood or oxygen.

With perfect liberty I would inspect Esteban's luxurious home, furnished at the expense of my father's life, taking note of windows, hallways, stairs—any detail that could contribute. I would attune myself to every passing remark, every hint of Esteban's habits and schedules.

In Madrid we transferred to a subway train. Less than an hour after setting out from Toledo we arrived at Atocha Station, near the Prado Museum and Retiro Park. The Sunday crowd was thick. As we strolled down the broad Paseo del Prado, tourists clicked pictures of the grand marble buildings and the fountains of Neptune and Apollo. Gypsies stationed themselves beneath the avenue's luscious trees. They ambushed gullible pedestrians with stories of woe. Naturally, they didn't waste their time on two penniless monks. But, all the same, I pulled a few pesetas from my pocket for a barefoot, bare-chested boy strumming a guitar.

By foot the walk to the Esteban estate took almost half an hour. Both of us were again soaked with sweat by the time we reached the front gate. A uniformed man inside a guardhouse buzzed open the gate and hurried out when he saw Bernardo. He was wiping his lips with a napkin.

"*Buenos Días*, Padre Bernardo!" Beaming, he embraced Bernardo.

"Not padre yet, Guillermo, only Brother. This is Padre Juan Ramón," Bernardo said, nodding toward me. "Guillermo has been with our family since before I was born."

"Thirty-five years, Padre," Guillermo boasted. He was a stocky man with a broad face and a bushy gray mustache full of crumbs from his lunch. "I have never missed a day guarding this house."

"Congratulations," I said.

"I will call for the driver," Guillermo said to Bernardo. He started for the guardhouse.

"No, Guillermo," Bernardo called. "We can walk to the house."

We started up the long, pine-lined drive. It wound through a thick verdant lawn that Esteban's gardener must have slaved to maintain. Ahead of us the mansion of stucco and brick nestled among more pines, the terra cotta roof a clean contrast to the deep green of the foliage. As we passed beneath the portico, one of the double doors opened.

"Welcome home, Padre Bernardo." The old servant wore a red coat. Unlike Guillermo, the reserved man made no attempt to embrace Bernardo.

"Thank you, Pedro. This is Father Juan Ramón."

The old man, who still stood straight as a soldier, nodded respectfully and turned to Bernardo. "The Señora waits for you in the front salon."

"We would like to wash up, Pedro. Please tell my mother we will join her shortly."

Pedro nodded and signaled to a maid in a black dress and white apron. She led us through the tall arches of the foyer to bathrooms where she furnished towels. The mirror and chrome faucet in my bathroom sparkled. So did the cool pink marble walls and floor. In the mirror I saw how flushed I was. I slipped off my habit and ran a cool cloth over my face and neck and over the dark hair of my chest and arms. It occurred to me that my body would impress Bernardo. Lifting weights had bubbled up my chest and thickened my biceps. I stuck my head under the faucet, toweled off, and raked my hair back with a pocket comb.

When I emerged from the bathroom, the maid, a thin,

glum looking woman in her forties, waited dutifully along-side Bernardo in the foyer. Standing next to him in her black dress, she reminded me of a sour nun from San Salvador. She led us back through the entrance hall into a large salon with glass doors that opened onto a terrace. A massive Persian rug covered the central section of the white marble tiles. Sofas and chairs upholstered in various shades of damask trimmed with gold piping formed several sitting areas, one around a stone fireplace. Above the mantle hung a life-size oil portrait of a fierce looking dowager, seated stiffly in an eggplant-colored dress, hands clasped on her lap. Her brilliant diamond ring was prominent, as were the diamonds in the cross suspended from a silver chain around her neck. The other oils on the bright walls had religious subjects. Bernardo later told me that they were antiques salvaged from Spanish churches after the Civil War.

Señora Esteban rose from an armchair by the fireplace when we entered.

"Bernardo." She smiled. She was slender in a silky violet dress. It struck me again that at 50 or so she was still a beautiful woman, with her high cheekbones, intelligent brow, and long slender neck. A tiny gold crucifix, half as large as the cross in the portrait, hung from a fine chain around her neck.

Bernardo embraced her. "You remember Father Juan Ramón, Mama," he said.

She held out her hand to me. "Welcome, Father. I am pleased to have you in our home." She seemed more at ease with me than she'd been at Santo Domingo. Of course, then, at my first sight of Esteban's wife, I'd probably been staring at her like some kind of pervert.

"The pleasure is mine, Señora." I clasped her hand.

She graciously bowed her head and motioned for us to take a seat on the sofa. She signaled to the maid, who had continued to stand at the entrance of the salon. The woman disappeared through the archway and returned in a few moments with a decanter of wine and glasses on a tray. Quietly and efficiently she poured a glass for each of us and once again slipped out of the room.

"I hope you enjoyed your visit to Santo Domingo last week, Señora," I said.

"Very much. I envy you, living in such a place. No distractions of the world. Here it's hard to escape them." She glanced about the room.

"Mother should have been a nun," Bernardo said. "As it is, she spends most of her time in church."

"Oh?" I guessed that her trips to church were probably an escape from the bastard she had married. She was, no doubt, of the old school, believing that her wifely duties included enduring her husband's abuse. According to Bernardo that took the form of backhanding most of the time, though occasionally she felt the force of Esteban's fist on her face.

"Don't be silly, Bernardo," she said. "I go to daily mass, Father, that's all."

"A commendable habit," I said. "Where do you go?"

"A convent nearby. The sisters sing the office first."

"A convent? Mass must be very early there." Esteban could be taken in the early morning hours as well as in the night. The Señora's absence from the house would make the work easier.

"Indeed. Six o'clock. The streets are still empty, thank

God." The Señora sipped her wine. "Bernardo tells me you're serving at Santiago del Arrabal, Father. I hope Bernardo is assigned to a church like that. Of course, all of Toledo's churches are beautiful. Not like the ones here in Madrid. In my mind they've been soiled by the awful Republicans who occupied them during the war."

"But Franco saved them," I said.

"Yes. Thank God for Franco."

"Bernardo tells me that you and Señor Esteban were great friends of the Generalissimo."

"I don't know about that. Franco had many, many friends."

"Mother is modest," Bernardo said. "Franco was our guest on a number of occasions."

"Bernardo's father knows many important people," the Señora explained, a trace of sadness rather than pride in her voice.

"What about Bernardo's father?"

The bass voice came from behind us. My blood shot through me like an undammed stream at the sound of it. As Bernardo stood so did I, turning to see Martin Esteban in person for the first time since that day more than 20 years before. His hair was gray at the temples and he was heavier now, in his dark suit. But the hard arrogance in his face had not changed.

"Hello, Father." Bernardo made no move to embrace Esteban. "This is my friend, Father Juan Ramón."

I extended my hand and Esteban clasped it in his own large, strong hand. "A pleasure to meet you, Father. So, you've been assigned to be Bernardo's protector. Someone needs to be." His eyes were as black as tar.

"Everyone needs a protector, Señor Esteban." I eyed my opponent. His gaze was level with mine.

Esteban laughed. "What a fellow, Bernardo. He'll be a good influence on you."

Bernardo remained silent.

"I believe dinner is ready," Esteban said. "Mama has been seated. Today is my mother's birthday, Father. She's 81. Humble stock, you know. She wasn't softened by all this luxury. But she likes it well enough now."

"I don't doubt it, Señor." I smiled for him. "Your home is exquisite."

"Thank you, Father. I'm quite proud of it." He motioned for his wife to lead the way to the dining room. She took Bernardo's arm and started across the salon. Esteban and I followed. "I'll tell you that all this is a testament to capitalism," Esteban continued. "Wealth is here for the taking, never doubt that. Of course, you monks don't care much for wealth, do you? All the more for us, I say."

"What, you don't already have it all?" I joked.

Esteban laughed again, uproariously, and slapped me on the back. "You're cut from different cloth than these other pious priests are, Father. Are you sure you've made the right career choice?"

"Oh, yes. Monks get to enjoy the fruits of you industrialists without any of the work. Not a bad deal, is it?"

"No, by God. It's not."

We found Esteban's mother already seated in the dining room. Though now frail and pallid and older by 15 years, she was clearly the model for the painting above the mantel. She brightened slightly when Bernardo kissed her and managed a weak smile when he introduced me to her.

"I am very honored to meet you, Señora." I strained to see in the old woman's dull eyes some explanation for her son's ruthlessness. But either her declining health had squelched its power, or she, like her daughter-in-law, held no authority over the conscience of Esteban.

When we were seated in the dining room, old Pedro poured our water and wine. Esteban sat at one end of the massive table and his wife at the other. I assumed the unhappy pair took these distant seats even when they ate alone—that is, if they took meals together at all. The table was covered in white linen. The crystal chandelier cascading over the table gleamed. So did the dishes. The fluted edges of the china and the rims of the glasses were gilded.

"I would like to make a toast," Bernardo said. He seemed quite at home in the elegant room, despite the deliberateness of his gesture. "To our guest, Juan Ramón, and to the family who welcomes him. May God bless us all."

"Here, here," Esteban said, perfunctorily, taking a gulp from his glass. "Drink up, Mama." He signaled to the old woman, who fumbled with her glass until Pedro assisted her. "I'm willing to bet they don't serve this wine at the monastery, Father. A Piedmont Barolo, vintage 1965."

"I don't know," I said. "We have some generous benefactors. Don't we, Bernardo?" I couldn't help feeling sorry for Bernardo, who seemed to be straining to contain his own disgust for Esteban.

"I suppose so," Bernardo said, quietly.

"Well, I won't be outdone. I'll send a case of something down to Toledo. Nothing too good, though. The best must be reserved for connoisseurs. Isn't there something in the Bible about casting pearls before swine?"

"Martin!" pleaded his wife.

"What? I'm quoting scripture, for God's sake." He laughed. "She takes everything too seriously. Doesn't she, Mama?"

The old woman's face remained blank, as though she hadn't heard him.

As the first course was served, an oppressive silence fell over the table. Esteban seemed oblivious to it. He sat back in his chair, wine in hand, like a king surveying his subjects.

I was satisfied with what I saw. The man was easy to hate, and he would be easy to kill.

Finally, Bernardo spoke. "How is business going, Father?"

"Business? Since when are you interested in business?"

"I'm making conversation." Bernardo's eyes flashed angrily.

"What an honor! I'm touched, Bernardo. Really, I am." Esteban stabbed a piece of veal with his fork and raised it to his mouth.

"Bernardo tells me you're in textiles," I said. "How did you get into that line?"

"Business savvy, Father." Esteban tapped his temple. "People will always buy clothing. And there will always be an international market—as long as we keep our costs down. We can produce a shirt for mere pesetas, then sell it at designer prices."

"With the help of slave labor," Bernardo said.

"Exactly, my boy." Esteban swallowed and wiped his mouth with his napkin. "The Basques are hard workers, and cheap."

"How long have you been in the business?" I said.

"Over 20 years. Remarkable, isn't it? You want to know the true key to my success, Father? Self-interest. Capitalism turns on it. You put your own interests first, and you'll find a way to be competitive. Drive your laborers. Find more efficient ways. Cut whatever corners you can. The market thrives. Spain thrives. The Church thrives. My son here hates to hear that."

"The Church thrives in poverty," Bernardo said, concentrating on his glass.

Esteban laughed. "A fairy tale. Keep believing it, Bernardo. Maybe they'll make you pope some day."

For the rest of the meal, Bernardo said little as his father waxed on. I listened with interest and continued asking questions that allowed Esteban to gloat. When dinner was finished I asked for a tour of the mansion. Naturally, the lord of the manor was happy to oblige his guest. And Bernardo seemed happy to retire to the salon with his mother and grandmother.

After Esteban had shown me a music room, a formal parlor, and a billiard room in the main wing of the house, he led him to a hallway off the foyer.

"These are my rooms, Father."

"They're not off limits?"

Esteban smiled. "Not for our special guests." He clapped me on the back and nodded for me to come with him down the hallway.

One side of the passage opened onto a pool, enclosed in an atrium. We walked around it and toured adjacent exercise rooms full of machines and weights and a sauna. After I showed I was duly impressed, Esteban led me to the opposite suite, where his office was located. One side of the huge room was a sitting area, containing sofas, armchairs, and a bar. The other side was a working area. In the middle of it was a desk nearly half as large as the dining room table. A computer rested on it. I noticed the shelves and cabinets that took up an entire wall. Photographs were scattered among the shelves. My attention was immediately drawn to one of my father and Esteban, standing before the entrance of their Basque textile plant. In order to inspect it more closely, I picked up a nearby photograph of Franco, the King, and Esteban.

"Impressive associates, Señor," I said.

"The Royal Palace is like a second home to me, Father," Esteban joked.

I continued holding the photograph while examining the one of my father. It must have been taken shortly before Esteban murdered him. In it my father was tall and dark. His expression and posture gave him an air of refinement without pretense. He was not strikingly handsome, though his face was full of strength and dignity. The sight of him summoned a familiar longing that cut through me like a jagged blade. How had such a man ever trusted Esteban? Perhaps he never had. But then he would have been foolish to continue as his business partner.

A quick scan of the other photographs did not reveal the actual executioners, but this didn't surprise me. Two henchmen were unlikely subjects for photographs on a rich executive's shelves.

"Please have a seat, Father."

I sat in the leather chair he indicated, and Esteban took a seat nearby, lighting a cigar. Sunlight pouring through the room's large windows sliced the smoke that swirled above his head.

"Would you like one?" Esteban said, holding up his cigar. "Or are monks permitted such luxuries?"

His expression in that moment contained a glimmer of something I'd seen that day from my parents' bedroom. A contemptuous air, a sense of superiority above moral laws and the common people who must abide by them.

"No, thank you, Señor. I do enjoy luxuries, but in other forms."

"Ah, spiritual riches. My wife and son talk about them. You seem to be in a different category, Father. Forgive me if I say it, but the habit doesn't become you."

"We all have our reasons, Señor." I wondered whether Esteban was mocking me. "Some take the habit out of guilt for the past. Others have saintly ambitions. My motives were different."

"Oh?" Esteban blew out a stream of smoke.

"The luxury I mentioned. In the monastery I have the luxury to think and dream, make my own plans, without having to worry about business or family affairs."

"What's the use of dreaming? I say grab what you want. That's what I've always done. That's why I have all this. And, believe me, I waste no time worrying about business or family. They depend on me, not the other way around."

"So, nothing ever scares you?"

Esteban tapped his cigar on an ashtray. "Why should I be scared, Father? I've got everything I want. And if I think of something else to want, I get it."

"What about death, Señor?"

"What about it? You priests like to use that as a secret weapon, when nothing else scares the peons into kneeling before you in the confessional. Don't get me wrong, Father. My gifts to the Church are generous. Frankly, I like the honors that come my way from the prelates in red. I believe the Holy Father even knows my name."

I nodded to show I was impressed. "So, you're prepared to die?"

"I'll tell you a secret, Father." Esteban leaned forward in his chair. "Every now and then, it occurs to me that maybe—*maybe*—there's a hell. But, you know, it never worries me, thanks to the good sisters who taught me. They used to say that just one confused cry for mercy within the mind of a dying man will open the gates of heaven to him."

"Very comforting."

"Don't tell me that you, a holy monk, don't believe that?"

I wished I had a gun pointed at Esteban's head to let him try out his theory. "I'll tell you what I believe, Señor. I believe that God is as hard and ruthless as a good industrialist, like you. That he loses no sleep over his accounts. They take care of themselves—debits, credits, payments, penalties. There are no magic words that allow the soul to circumvent the divine system."

Esteban laughed. "Oh, Father. Here I thought you were different from the others. But you're a true-blue monk. It's just your demeanor that's different. Still, I can't help liking you."

"I'm honored, Señor."

"You should be. I don't care for many people. Frankly, I don't care for anyone who's afraid of me. Even though they should be. You're not afraid of me. Tell me, Father, why is that?"

I shrugged. "Maybe I understand you."

"I believe you do." Esteban seemed amused. "But how can that be, Father? How can a monk understand someone like me? Someone—how did you put it?—ruthless and hard, the way God is too, according to your theory. Unless you're just as much like God as I am. Is that it?"

"God has carried out his designs through many unworthy agents over the course of history. Even some as unworthy as me."

Clenching his cigar in his teeth, Esteban laughed hard. Then he laid the cigar in the ashtray. "I've been called many things, Father, but never an agent of God. Of course we were referring to you, weren't we? So perhaps I am ruthless as Satan and you are the one like God. That sounds more like it, wouldn't you say? At any rate, I'll take my chances on a split-second confession before the angel of death carries me away."

After more banter, Esteban escorted me back to the salon and out to the terrace. The gardens below were a mass of patterned colors, like *las alfombras*, the confetti carpets spread down the aisles of Mexican churches during Holy Week. The warm air smelled like pine. Maybe this beautiful scene had stretched before Esteban as he planned the murders? Or maybe he came here to recover afterward? No, I decided, Esteban was not the type to reflect or recover. He simply made plans and executed them. He was a man of the moment. Besides, even nature belonged to him, and a man doesn't contemplate property.

Once we'd said our goodbyes, Esteban had his driver take us to Atocha.

Bernardo stewed on the train ride back. Was he torturing himself because he'd acted like a fucked-over son instead of a saint? Or did he just want some attention? He shot me a wounded glance a couple of times. Maybe he was jealous that Papa had taken to his irreverent friend? I almost broke out laughing at the irony of it. Then, sitting there, taking in Bernardo's lithe body, his pretty profile as he gazed out the window, something came to me. At the time I thought it was just a fantasy. Now I know it was already something more. I'd always planned to use Bernardo to get to Esteban. Somehow win the bastard's trust through his son, insert myself into his world until the right moment came to strike. My original thoughts were of getting Bernardo to make up with Papa. But there was a better way, I realized suddenly, a perfect way. What if Bernardo was the one to cut him? A *maricon* did amazing things for a lover. Especially a trusting, idealistic puppy like Bernardo.

"I take it the visit home disappointed you?" I said to break the silence.

Bernardo continued staring out the window without answering.

"You can't expect immediate success, you know." I squeezed his leg.

"It's impossible. The whole thing. You've seen what high regard my father has for me. We have as much chance at getting along as Communists and the Church."

"You being the Church?"

The comment apparently hit a nerve. Bernardo finally turned and glared at me. "Yes, I'm proud. And yes, I resent him. I guess I'm not advanced enough in spiritual perfection to accept him. The best I can do is keep out of his way. At least then I keep myself from wishing he was dead. Imagine, a professed monk wanting his father dead!"

"Come on, Bernardo," I coaxed. "You've taken the first

step. You're admitting the truth. No campaign is effective unless the general correctly assesses the obstacles—including the weaknesses in his own men."

The anger faded from Bernardo's strabismic eyes, replaced by a sweet sort of helplessness. He swallowed and opened his mouth to speak, a thread of saliva joining his lips. But he just sighed and turned back to the window.

We arrived at Santo Domingo as the monastery bell was summoning the monks to chapel. We went directly to vespers and then on to supper. During the meal I threw encouraging glances at Bernardo.

When the Grand Silence began, I went to my stuffy cell, stripped, and waited in the dark. I paced and went to the window to catch some air and paced some more. I sat on the bed and rubbed my cock and imagined Bernardo's white ass. When the chapel bell chimed 11 o'clock, I threw on a terry cloth robe and padded down the cool corridor floors to Bernardo's cell on the opposite side of the courtyard. He answered right away when I knocked, probably unable to sleep.

"Juan Ramón?" he said. "What's wrong?"

It took a few seconds for my eyes to adjust from the corridor's dim lighting to the pitch black room. I went over and opened the curtains to let in some light from the plaza below. I stood in front of the window where Bernardo could see me and whipped off my robe.

He sat up on the bed. "My God," he said.

"What?" I said. "Are you impressed?"

He looked toward the door.

"Don't go anywhere, Bernardo."

I pushed him back onto his bed, worked off his briefs.

He was hard. I licked his smooth chest, his excited nipples, tongued my way down to his cock, his balls, his thighs. Soccer thighs, I discovered—full and firm. I groped his arms. Not bulky, but hard all the same, muscular. Straddling his chest, I propped his pillow under his head and guided him to my balls. He sucked like a hungry baby. I fucked his mouth until I was ready to shoot, then pulled out and flipped him over.

"Stay there," I said. I got a tube of lubrication from my robe pocket, greased myself up, and mounted him from behind.

"You want it, *maricon*?" I bent over and bit his ear, my hard flesh sliding along his crack.

"Yes," he said into his pillow.

"*Muy bien.*" I pressed against his tight sphincter, then rammed myself in. He groaned. He fit me tight as a sausage casing. *The bastard's faggoty son*, I thought. Esteban's arrogant face flashed through my mind. I pumped, stopped, pumped. I flipped him over, leaned down to find his warm mouth. I crammed in my tongue and he sucked hard. His spit drenched my goatee. I chewed at his lips, reached down and squeezed his cock.

"Get up," I said. "Kneel."

He knelt on the bed, braced himself against the headboard. I drilled him again, reached around to work his cock. When I felt his belly quivering against my forearm, I emptied myself into him. He moaned and my hand was warm with his cum. I collapsed on his back, still in him, and stayed there until my heart quit pounding.

Eight

BERNARDO

Water puddled in the Plaza Ayuntamiento. The rain had ended before dawn, but it left the shaded lower half of the cathedral darker than the top, as though the river had flooded its banks and risen to the stone galleries before receding. Juan Ramón breathed through his mouth. I closed my mouth for a moment to listen to him inhaling and exhaling with a perfectly even rhythm. I watched his white, mud-streaked running shoes pound the bricks.

"Come on," he said. "Once around the cathedral. Hard."

We sprinted past the treasury side and around the back. When he dodged a girl on a bicycle, I took the lead. My heartbeat accelerated as I turned the corner, the plaza spread out before me. His dark legs flashed beside me, then his gray shorts. His feet kicked up furiously behind him as he passed me. I leaned forward, pushed myself, reached into myself for reserved fuel. My elbow brushed his as I passed him. I hurdled the puddle and stopped. He landed beside me. We both bent over, hands on our knees, gasping for air.

We walked for a while in silence. Shopkeepers were propping their doors open, sweeping the sidewalks. In a side street that was still quiet, Juan Ramón clasped my arm, pulled me to him, and kissed me. His lips and beard were salty from sweat.

"Come with me to Santiago today," he said. "Simon wants me to sort out the parish files. He likes you."

It was a school holiday. Some of the staff members had taken the students camping out on the *meseta*.

"All right," I said. Anything to spend the day with him. When I was with him, everything seemed right. We belonged together. No doubts. No guilt. They were for the lonely moments. And for the moment at the communion rail as I stretched out my tongue to receive the sacred host—in the state of mortal sin. But I had to receive or the others would know.

We ran into Baroja in the entrance hall as we were leaving the monastery for Santiago.

"Here they are," he said, "the young blood of Santo Domingo." His arms were crossed under his scapular. "Isn't this a school holiday, Bernardo?"

"I'm helping Juan Ramón organize parish records."

Baroja smiled. "Better man than I. You've got yourself a true friend, Juan Ramón."

Juan Ramón nodded.

Outside, Juan Ramón said, "He's happy we've hit it off. Don't you think so?"

I shrugged.

"What's wrong?"

"If he knew…"

"If he knew, we'd be lectured, disciplined, and separated. End of story. But he doesn't need to know."

"It doesn't bother you?"

"I've told you. You're thinking small, like Eduardo. Don't put God in a box."

"But it's a contradiction."

Juan Ramón stopped walking and grabbed my shoulder when I stopped. "Contradictions are for people who see everything as black and white." He glanced up the street and sighed. "*Muy bien*, Bernardo. Maybe you can't see it. But trust me, will you. Will you?"

I nodded.

At Santiago we spent the morning in Simon's office. I arranged two file drawers of baptismal certificates in chronological order. Juan Ramón worked on the marriage certificates. We sat across from each other at a table we'd carried in from the foyer. The housekeeper brought us some tea. We'd been working about an hour when Juan Ramón started to laugh.

"What?"

He couldn't stop laughing and just handed me a photograph. It was a wedding picture. The groom wore regalia from the order of the Knights of Columbus, a tricorn hat with a plume, a cape, and a stripped ribbon across his chest. The stocky bride grinned stupidly, not a tooth in her mouth.

When Juan Ramón drew his lips under his teeth and smiled to imitate the bride, I laughed so hard I had to run to the bathroom.

• • •

I couldn't keep my promise to Juan Ramón. Some nights I woke up racked with guilt. Finally, I had to confess. At the cathedral, I dipped my fingers into the holy water and made the sign of the cross. Just inside the Watch Door. *In el nombre del Padre, del Hijo, del Espíritu Santo*, Sweet Jesus help me! The cool church was a relief from the sweltering day. I paused to let my eyes adjust to the darkness. I walked to the chancel and knelt before the smiling *Virgen Blanca*, her wooden face painted rosy beige. Her child, nestled in her arms and touching her round chin, smiled too. But neither smile made it all better. I bowed my head to examine my conscience.

How long since my last confession? Three weeks? Three weeks of him riding me, stroking me, piercing and pounding me. He'd broken me in the way an Argentine gaucho breaks in a colt that prances to a cliff and sneers down at a corral of horses, mating and grazing in their own manure. I fit him now all the way into my belly. The wrong words kept coming to me, words that took me to another butte above the mesa, but not alone: *And let us go forth to behold ourselves in your beauty, to the mountain and to the hill, to where the pure water flows...to the high caverns in the rock...there you will show me what my soul has been seeking*. Words from *Dark Night*, words about my Beloved. But who was he? Hot lust was blinding me. Tears as warm as

Juan Ramón's rich seed came to my eyes and spilled down my face. The *Virgen Blanca's* beige face blurred.

I found the special confessional where priests from out of town were assigned. Anonymity might help me.

"Bless me, Father, for I have sinned." I crossed myself. The darkness of the box was like my own dark cell at night before I fell asleep, but today it was not comforting. "It has been three weeks since my last confession. I am a monk." A monk had to identify himself, according to our novice master. A confessor must know how to weigh sins so as to give the right penance. The same sin committed by a monk and a layman was not really the same sin.

"Proceed, my son." The voice was old, raspy.

I sucked in a breath. "I'm not sure where to start, Father. Everything is so chaotic. I want to dedicate myself to the way of perfection, to surrender to God."

"This is your calling as a professed monk." The old priest spoke in a matter-of-fact way. "So why the chaos?"

Say it, I told myself. *Say it and save everything.* I tried, but the wrong sin got in the way.

"I know I should love my father," I said. "But when I'm in his house, I feel...I hate him. I come back to the monastery a hypocrite."

"Why do you hate your father?"

"He's arrogant and selfish. He's a tyrant at his factories, and with my mother...he beats her, Father."

"And where do you enter into this behavior?"

My eyes filled. "It's my pride, Father, isn't it?" *Pride that I had conquered* him? *Pride that he wanted me?*

"Pride is an insidious thing, my son," the old man said. "It hides our real motives. You go to your father to prove you are capable of forgiving him, to prove you can master hatred. No wonder chaos enters your soul. You must be true to your vocation. It is your path to sanctity. The monk lives in quiet. He is not a missionary or a social worker. Surrender this ambition to master your father and yourself. Pray for forgiveness. Pray for humility."

"Yes, Father." I bowed my head.

"Is there more?"

My heart hammered at my ribs. I squeezed my clammy palms together. The dark confessional felt close and hot. "Yes, Father," I said.

The old man shifted.

"I have…attractions…unnatural attractions, Father. To another monk." My face got hot with embarrassment. *Not the first time to confess this*, I told myself, *Not the first time. And you're only starting. He'll ask it now.* And he did.

"Have you acted on these attractions?" His voice was grave. "I said, have you acted?"

"Yes."

The old man gasped. "*Dios, Hijo! Dios!*" He mumbled to himself what seemed like an incantation to ward off evil.

"And your brother?"

"My brother?"

"Has he encouraged this?" he said impatiently.

"Yes."

"*Dios!*" He thought for a moment. When he spoke again his voice was calmer but more deliberate and urgent. "The devil does his best to ruin those with a religious calling. He preys on solitude and loneliness. Men can resort to unnatural acts they have never considered. In the name of brotherly love, you must end this friendship. Go to your spiritual director. Ask him to petition the abbot for a transfer to another monastery. Before it is too late."

Too late?.O Cristo!

"Do you understand?"

"Yes, Father."

"Trust me, my son. Physical separation is the only answer. You can't rely on your own will power."

He assigned me a rosary for my penance, absolved me, and slammed the panel shut.

Nine

Juan Ramón

The trip to Esteban's house fucked up my mind. I was obsessed with the bastard. I kept seeing his arrogant grin as he leaned against his desk, the cigar clenched in his teeth. Within my reach. I could have jumped up and strangled him then and there. He was a big man but flabby and over 50. There was no way I could lose. And I just fucking sat there, making smart talk so he could be amused by the savvy monk.

The picture of him in his office got mixed up in my mind with the image of him giving the nod to the canine Castro straddling my mother on the bedroom floor. I remembered

Esteban's big hands clutching me, keeping me from going to my mother. I remembered the smell of cigars lingering on the bastard's wool suit. "Do the hell what you want." *Claro*, he was a fucking busy man with things to do. Get it all the hell over with, as if my mother was some kind of ride in Retiro Park.

My daytime obsessions worked their way into my sleep. I had a dream about my mother. She was screaming my name. *Juan Ramón! Don't you love Mama?* I struggled to see her through the window of the balcony outside our apartment, but it was obstructed with strings of pearls that formed a bead curtain. Crazed, I tugged at the door, but it wouldn't budge. I pounded the glass and called her name. Neighbors gathered below to watch me, laughing and pointing. They were not the tiny specks they'd been when I used to gaze down from our penthouse apartment: Somehow the apartment had moved to a floor near ground level.

Help me! I yelled. *A man is murdering my mama!* I stood with clenched fists at my sides, wanting to pounce like a cat on the spectators just standing there, gawking.

Where is your father? Why isn't he helping her? a sour-faced old woman cried up to me. She was shading her eyes from the morning sun.

I didn't know what the hell to answer. Where was my father?

Just then two paramedics wheeled a gurney out the entrance of the apartment building. The man on the gurney wore a suit. His face was a blur. It occurred to me that this could be my father.

Papa! I called over the balustrade.

One of the paramedics glanced up and grinned as though he was an old friend of the family who could communicate with a mere expression. *Where's your mama, Juan Ramón?* he seemed to be saying.

I started pounding the glass again, as my mother called my name. Then there was silence. I pressed my ear to the glass but heard nothing. I turned to the balustrade and waited for the second gurney. It rolled out of the building without the help of attendants, as though it was on automatic pilot. My mother was stretched out, her black dress splattered with crimson, her face as white as milk.

Mama! I cried.

My mother opened her eyes, threw me a recriminating glance, and closed them again as the gurney rolled down the street.

A bell clanged. I woke up. The cell was dark. Outside the door, a bass voice sang, *"Benedicite Dominum."* It was Brother Vicente, making the morning rounds with his hand bell. A rap followed. My body was damp with perspiration. I went to the open window and stuck out my head for air. I decided I couldn't wait to kill the bastard. I couldn't let Bernardo have the pleasure—that is if that pious *maricon* could ever be pushed into the deed. Maybe I was fucking deluded about my power over him. Fuck the plans. Fuck the caution. I had to have Esteban now. I'd waited long enough.

That night after 11 o'clock, I groped around in the monastery's dark kitchen for a knife. I found one with a blade about as long as my hand and dropped it into my satchel. I let myself out the side door at the entrance of the chapel. At the Toledo station I waited in the shadows until a train came and climbed into an empty car.

Traffic was heavy on the Paseo del Prado, even at midnight. The *Madrileños* kept late hours at the theaters, restaurants, and shops around the Plaza Mayor. I hustled past the museum and the illuminated fountain of Neptune, water gushing around the feet of the dark god. By the time I arrived on Esteban's street my back was sopping through my T-shirt. I'd slipped into the T-shirt and a pair of jeans because at that hour my habit would have drawn attention. At Esteban's gate, a dim light glowed in the guardhouse. I could make out Guillermo's stocky form. He was dozing, his head back against the wall and his hands clasped over his stomach.

I crept along the iron pales, trying to stay in the line of tall pines along the fence in case Guillermo woke up. I positioned myself before Esteban's wing. Although the distance between me and the mansion was about the length of a soccer field, I could see lights in Esteban's office and in his bedroom at the end of the wing, where Esteban hadn't taken me during his visit. It was nearly 1 o'clock. The rest of the house was dark. Did Esteban work this late every night? Was he alone?

I sat down against a tree and watched for nearly half an hour until the lights in the office went off. Within 10 minutes a red sports car drove up the street to the gate. Someone tapped the horn and Guillermo roused himself, yawning. The gate eased back and the sports car rolled through. Guillermo watched it as it made its way down the drive to the entrance of the mansion. I couldn't make out the driver.

Evidently the visitor was let in through the front door.

I kept my eye on Esteban's bedroom. The light remained steady for some time, then dimmed to almost nothing.

I waited a good hour. When I finally gave up and got up

to go, the sports car moved. I crept closer to the guardhouse and saw that chunky Guillermo had nodded off again. I passed the gate and crouched down behind some hedges in front of the guardhouse to give myself the best possible view of the driver's side of the car. The horn beeped. The gate slid open. The woman behind the wheel had long white-blond hair, undoubtedly bleached. Her skin was dark against it. Her shoulders were bare, her long red fingernails prominent on the steering wheel. She might have been 30, judging from her profile. An expensive whore making her regular rounds, starting with her best client.

I realized how fucked up I was, thinking I would toss out all my plans, all the waiting, all the years, and come and rashly take out Esteban. Then what? Spend my life in a rank Madrid prison for him? When enough time had elapsed to let Guillermo fall back, I stood and started to make my way to the quiet street that connected the estates surrounding the Retiro Park.

"Who's there?" Guillermo called after me.

I knew that unless he was on top of me, he would never recognize me as the monk who came for a Sunday visit with Bernardo. Without changing my pace, I kept walking, my face toward the street.

"Stop, Señor! I said stop!"

Guillermo's voice was closer now. I couldn't believe the overweight guard would bother running after me.

"I have a gun. I will fire it, Señor!"

A ruse, I thought. But rather than chance it, I sprinted away into the shadows of the street. Dogs barked behind the fence of a neighboring mansion. I kept running until I was well past the entrance of Retiro Park.

Ten

BERNARDO

My fate with Juan Ramón was sealed at San Servando one beautiful day a week after my confession. The sky stretched clear and azure above the soccer field where two teams of boys charged toward the goal of the yellow shirts.

I was in shorts and a T-shirt and the breeze felt good on my skin. I let my gaze wander above the action to the blue vault. San Servando's white towers cut into it, and down and beyond the orphanage so did Toledo's jagged ochre skyline. The cathedral spire made me think about the confession. I'd played the priest's counsel over and over and over in my mind. *It isn't Juan Ramón*, I kept saying to myself. *It really isn't. It's the boys at San Servando. To leave Toledo, to leave the boys. How can I do it?*

Whenever a voice from the game strayed from the normal cheers or curses, my attention went immediately to the field. Lately there had been too much trouble with Tomás, a misfit. I couldn't trust even the good boys to leave him alone anymore.

I strained to locate the short 14-year-old among the red shirts flashing across the field. He was a quick boy, but the others still refused to pass him the ball much. Now, as a lanky boy on the red team guided the ball to one corner of the field with an eye to the goal, Tomás surfaced from the mob of arms and legs and signaled to his teammate. He was open and clear. He shouted *"Pasame!"* in his high-pitched voice, waving his skinny arms above him. Alfredo ignored him, aiming instead a virtually impossible shot directly at the goal. The stocky yellow goalie rebuffed the ball with his chest and one of the yellows kicked it down the field toward the red goal. Tomás hung back when his teammates raced to the defense. He watched, both hands in fists, then sprinted back to the game.

This was typical. The boys had never accepted Tomás, even after their unofficial (and forbidden) initiation period of roughhousing and harassing. Boys who didn't whine or inform during the rites were usually welcomed into the pack. But not Tomás. He had too much going against him from the very beginning. On the third day of class, I had called on him to read. A look of alarm spread across his broad face and he froze. I realized he couldn't read. My remorse must have shown because the boys took it as pity and started jeering. Somebody launched an eraser at him. He shoved the Bible off his desk, sprang up, and started swinging his fists at the face of the boy across the aisle. Miguel and a few other boys jumped from their desks to pull him away. Before I could get to him, Tomás spit at Miguel, yanked himself from his grasp, and ran out of the room.

The news of Tomás's illiteracy had spread quickly. The cruelty was relentless. I confronted Miguel one day.

"I am disappointed to see this in you," I'd said. Miguel was tying his cleated soccer shoe on a bench in the locker room. His bare leg was tan and solid, the calf bulging above the white sock. I liked him, and Miguel knew it. He could usually be trusted to keep the others in line. But a misguided integrity had turned him into a Nazi.

"He brings it on himself," Miguel retorted, reeling back his mop of shaggy hair and scowling. Don't put this on me or anybody else, Brother. He's a shit."

"Tomás can't read, Miguel. It embarrasses him."

"It should."

"He had to take care of his crippled father. He couldn't go to school." I'd learned this from a representative of the state agency that had sent Tomás to San Servando.

"And he's an orphan. You see me weeping, Brother?" Miguel lowered his foot to the floor and straightened, crossing his bare arms and eyeing me resentfully. The clear whites of his eyes against his brown face said health and youth, and even purity—like that of steel or of hard clean pine, not of soul.

"I'm not asking you to pity him."

"Good thing." Miguel turned and grabbed an athletic

cup from his open locker. He slipped it into his gym shorts, slammed the metal door, and jogged off down the hallway.

So the boy I could usually count on not only failed to restrain himself but half the time became an instigator of the abuse.

Unacceptable cries from the field suddenly caught my attention. The boys had crowded around a fight near the red goal. I ran to the scene and pushed through the sweaty bodies. My fears were confirmed. Tomás was struggling on the ground with one of the bigger boys, a 15-year-old named Jorge. The two interlocked bodies rolled around several times on the grass before I could reach them. Then Jorge managed to wedge Tomás's head in the crook of his arm. Their bodies formed a right angle. Blood rushed to Tomás's face. He started choking.

"Let him go, Jorge!" I yelled above the cheers of the boys. "I said let him go."

The round-headed Jorge looked up at me and started to let go. Then Tomás reached back and cuffed him in the face, and Jorge tightened his hold. Tomás seemed to go limp. I knelt and gripped Jorge's arm to pry it off. A sudden, sharp pain in my wrist made me let go. Blood dribbled from above my wristwatch down my fingers. Tomás drew back his hand to stab me again with a Swiss army knife that he must have had in his pocket.

"Get out of the way, Bernardo!" It was Juan Ramón. He must have walked to San Servando after finishing his duties at Santiago. He shoved me aside. He knelt down and grabbed Tomás's arm. He squeezed until the knife dropped to the ground. Tomás scrambled to recover it, but Juan Ramón tightened his hold. I snatched the knife.

"Let go of him," Juan Ramón yelled at Jorge.

Jorge released his hold of Tomás and stood.

Juan Ramón pulled Tomás to his feet and wrenched his arm behind his back. Tomás struggled to get loose, but he was no match for Juan Ramón. Every time Tomás kicked or tugged, Juan Ramón wrenched his arm harder until tears came to Tomás's wide-set eyes.

"That's right," Juan Ramón said through clenched teeth. "Move again, and I'll break your arm."

The other boys quietly gawked at Juan Ramón and Tomás.

"All right," I said to them. "Everyone inside."

They stayed there, frozen.

"You heard him," Juan Ramón said. "Now!"

As chastened as soldiers after a defeat, the boys solemnly trudged back to the building.

"Are you all right?" Juan Ramón said to me.

I had stuck the knife in my pocket and was putting pressure on my wrist. The wound wasn't deep but the blood still oozed. I nodded that I was OK.

"What should I do with him?"

Tomás had quit struggling. He was glaring at me, tears streaming down his face.

"Let him go," I said.

"He needs the shit knocked out of him."

"Let him go."

Juan Ramón released Tomás. He rubbed his arm and took off running down the hillside toward the city. "I hate you," he shouted over his shoulder.

"Let me see." Juan Ramón took my arm. He was wearing his habit, now strewn with grass. He pulled a white handkerchief out of the pocket and tied a tourniquet around my wrist. "They'll kill you, you know. One of these days." The look he flashed me was angry, but his touch was tender.

• • •

Three separate times after that day, I stood at my spiritual director's door. But I could never make myself knock. I kept thinking, *How can I abandon Tomás and the other boys?* Now, of course, I know the boys were an excuse, as much as they meant to me. It was Juan Ramón all along. I already belonged to him. But I wouldn't let myself see the danger.

Instead of leaving Santo Domingo, I decided to steer clear of Juan Ramón. Until my feelings died. I thought maybe I was letting my pride take over, but at least no one but me would have to suffer for it. That's what I told myself. *God*, I prayed, *please help me let go of him.* But in my heart I was praying, *Please, never take him away from me!*

Eleven

JUAN RAMÓN

I first noticed Bernardo's strange new reserve during vespers one evening. Normally I could catch his eye and smile when the old monks tripped over phrases like "shattering ships of Tarshish," in psalm 48 or when they belted out psalm 1's melodramatic "not so with the wicked, not so!" But Bernardo's gaze remained fixed on his breviary. Then during the recreation period he stuck around the others and spit out the obligatory shit about weather and upcoming jubilees and parishioners. He wouldn't let me get him off in a corner alone, and I could see he was afraid of himself more than me. The pious

monk felt guilty for fucking around; I knew the story—
I'd led other pretty celibates to the fiery brink and seen
them scramble for sanctuary, against their own appetite
for a shaft up their asses.

So I wasn't worried or surprised by his retreat. What *did*
surprise me was the moment I kept replaying in my head: that
fish-eyed brat sticking Bernardo with a knife. When I saw
that I wanted to twist off his head. If it had meant throwing
myself on top of Bernardo to keep the blade from finding him
again, I would have done it. That's what surprised me. And
scared me. Wanting Bernardo's smooth, plump ass, his delicate throat, his sweet balls nestled between soccer thighs—
that was sheer lust, mixed with the urge to fuck the hell out
of what belonged to Esteban. But wanting to protect him?
That messed up everything I was about.

I figured the sentiment was some perverse by-product of
my hatred for Esteban. Maybe I wanted to save Bernardo
from him.

After breakfast one morning I knocked on Bernardo's
door when I knew he'd be preparing for classes. He called for
me to come in. I found him at his desk, grading papers. He
looked up, steeling himself, I could see, against tenderness.

I sat on the bed, facing his profile. "I've missed you."

"Thank you for leaving me to myself."

I nodded toward his bandaged wrist. "How's the little bastard doing? Did you stick him in San Servando's dungeon?"

"I'm trying to place him in a foster home."

"Some trick that'll be. Hope you're a damned good liar."

Bernardo shrugged and looked at his papers.

I studied him for a minute then got up and peered out
the window. Down in the plaza a woman was pushing a

baby stroller toward a bench where two other women sat with their carriages.

"What are you doing, Bernardo?" I said without turning to him.

He didn't answer me, and I asked the question again.

"You know," he finally said.

"*Claro.* You've decided to abandon me." I shot him a look.

"No." He shook his head. "I wouldn't do that."

"Like hell. Don't play games with me."

"We're under vows. Doesn't that mean anything to you?"

"No good, Bernardo. All you care about is protecting your ordination."

"What do you want from me?" Anger flashed in his green eyes, accentuating the strabismus.

I resumed my seat on the bed. "You ever think about who Christ really was, Bernardo? Not some pious prig who obeyed the rules. He took risks, got himself killed."

"For our salvation."

I snorted. "For bucking the system. The whole hypocritical, oppressive system that made some people kings and others peons. The goddamn web of legalism. You think he cared about what happened in the bedroom? Hell, he probably would have screwed the woman caught in adultery, the one he saved from stoning, remember?"

"That's blasphemy."

"*Sí, verdad.* His brand of it."

Tears welled in his eyes and he looked away from me. "*O Dios!* I can't do this."

I reached over and grabbed his arm. "You don't have to *do* anything. Just let it happen."

He turned to me. "What kind of future can we have?"

"Where's your imagination? Where's your trust? What kind of a God do you worship? All things are possible, *que no*? And don't tell me the promise applies only to servile, scared idiots under the thumb of Holy Mother Church."

He sighed. "I don't know. I don't know anymore."

"Do you love me, Bernardo?"

"God, yes. I wish I didn't."

"So it's more than just lust. Did you ever think God put us together?"

"To ruin us?"

I shrugged. "You mean to take all this away? The holy walls? The secure cloister of Santo Domingo?"

"Sanctity. Salvation. That's what I mean."

"And I'm telling you to think bigger."

He was quiet for a moment. Then he threw me a sheepish look. "What about you?" he said.

"Me?"

"Do you love *me?*"

"I really have to say it? Why am I in this room? Why haven't I just written you off?" I stood and pulled him to his feet. I grabbed him by the chin and looked at him hard and long. His moist eyes were full of trust. I had him. But I didn't feel like a victor. I kissed him deeply, pulling him to me, hard with desire. In all of 10 minutes I had him stripped, mounted, and oozing with me. And when I left him, part of me stayed behind.

• • •

In the sacristy of Santiago del Arrabal a few days later, I was stuck getting things ready for mass. I poured wine from the bottle into a glass cruet and filled another cruet with water. I dropped a large communion wafer into a gold ciborium, placed a paten on the ciborium and then a square piece of cardboard covered in linen. I draped the vessels with the green cloth used during the ordinary season of the Church year. I put everything on a tray and carried it out to a side table in the sanctuary. The gray predawn light sifted through the tall gothic windows. In the cavernous church, only 10 or 12 people knelt in the pews, most of them old women in scarves but also a young couple who'd recently married. Automatically I genuflected before the tabernacle. I lit the candles standing near the altar and on the reredos at each side of the tabernacle. Then I switched on the lights above the sanctuary and the nave.

I resented playing altar boy for the doddering Simon. But the old idiot insisted on presiding at the early Sunday mass—despite the fact that he was still recovering from a virus that had nearly done him in. He wobbled on his legs like a baby just starting to walk. He couldn't manage a single move without me.

As I positioned the big-print lectionary on the pulpit, I heard the old man fumbling in the sacristy. I went back in and found him tugging at an alb caught on a hanger. His small, stooped frame was dwarfed by the oak wardrobe.

"Wait, Father," I said. "Those are the large albs. Let me." I snatched the hanger from the old man and removed another from the wardrobe, slipping off the alb and pulling it over Simon's head. "No, here, Father. Here's the sleeve." He might as well have been a 2-year-old.

After I tied the braided cincture around his waist and draped him with the green chasuble, I put on my own identical vestments. The inefficiency of it all—two priests for one mass—annoyed me, but what choice did I have? After he bowed to the crucifix above the wardrobe, I yanked the cord near the door, which rang a tiny bell in the sanctuary. I guided him by the elbow to the altar. The old man bowed instead of genuflecting, something I'd finally gotten him to do, and moved to the chair. He made the sign of the cross, extended his frail arms, leaned toward the microphone and addressed the congregation, "*El Señor sia con vosotros.*" His thin voice crackled through the speakers.

I read the Old Testament reading, the psalm, and the epistle from the lectern, then escorted Simon to the pulpit. He managed to read the Gospel, coughing and losing his place half a dozen times. I was able to relax for a few minutes when he proceeded on to the sermon. I started thinking about the Madrid phone directory I'd noticed in the porter's office at Santo Domingo. I was itching to look up the addresses of Castro and Entralgo. Over the years, whenever I was in Madrid, I made it a point to check the directory for their names. The problem with Castro was that at any given time there seemed to be four or five entries with the same name. Twice I called all the numbers until I thought I'd identified my Castro, but addresses change and I might have lost him. And I'd never found a listing for Umberto Entralgo. I prayed to God he was still alive.

When it came time for the Eucharistic prayer, I directed Simon to the altar and stood at his side as he recited the consecration. At the end of the consecration, when he blurted "*Benedito el que viene en el nombre del Señor,*" I interrupted him.

"No Father, it's too early for the *Sanctus*. The doxology, the doxology."

Simon blinked at me through his thick lenses.

"Through Him, With Him, In Him," I prompted in a whisper.

Like a parrot, Simon took up the words, elevating the host above the chalice. He received communion himself, then instead of waiting while I received it, started over to the chair unescorted, one unsure foot before the other. I hurried, but before I could reach him, he stumbled and fell. When I tried to help him up he moaned. I knew he'd sprained or broken his goddamned foot. I picked him up, amazed at how light he was, and carried him to the presider's chair. After distributing communion and finishing the mass myself, I removed the old man's vestments in the sanctuary and carried him to the old Volvo that he hadn't driven himself since I'd been stationed at Santiago. I managed to get him into the back seat then headed toward the Puerta de la Bisagra.

"Where are you going!" he whimpered as we turned north after passing through Bisagra.

"To San Rosario."

"No, take me to San Francisco. You'll miss the 11 o'clock mass."

"I'm taking you to Madrid, to a real hospital. We can be back in time."

During the 45-minute drive to Madrid, Simon dozed. I glanced at him whenever he groaned. He was pale and his forehead was screwed up in pain. Then sweat beaded on his head. I reached back and felt his cheek. It was warm. He probably had a mild fever, probably still had the flu. I fumbled with the top button of his cassock, but I couldn't get it undone and he pushed my hand away.

"*Muy bien*," I said. "Suit yourself." I quit trying and turned up the air conditioner.

At the hospital I left Simon outside the emergency room while I went in for help. A couple of stocky orderlies followed me out with a wheelchair, lifted the old man into it, and rolled him inside to an examining room. While he was being treated, a skinny nurse with bleached hair gathered the necessary information from me, pecking at the computer.

"Can't we hurry this up?" I said. A mistake. She turned resentful, suddenly repeating questions and fumbling even worse at the keyboard—if that was possible.

"How long will he be here, do you think?" I said.

She pretended not to hear me. I asked again, trying to be polite. I wanted to get to a phone book.

"It depends, Father," she said, glancing up from the computer. "His foot will be x-rayed. If it's broken they will set it and put it in a cast. From the looks of him, he may also be dehydrated. The doctor might wish to admit him."

According to the clock on the wall behind the nurse, it was already nearly 10 o'clock. I wouldn't be able to make it back for the 11 o'clock mass. So after finishing with the nurse, I found the pay phones and called the housekeeper to let her know what had happened.

"*O Dios!*" she said. "I told him he wasn't well yet, Father. Honestly, I did. But he can be so stubborn."

"Never mind, Elena." I imagined the plump old woman spending the rest of the day wringing her apron and pacing the floor. "You need to post a sign on the front door of the church that there won't be an 11 o'clock mass." It was too late to find someone to replace me. Every able-bodied priest at the monastery had Sunday duties somewhere, and I didn't know any other priest.

"I don't know, Father," Elena whimpered.

"It's only a note, Elena. Like the kind you leave me about food in the refrigerator."

"What should it say?"

I sucked in a deep breath to calm myself. "Write that the 11 o'clock mass is canceled."

"But what if people come to the rectory? What should I say?"

"Just tell them what happened."

"What about your lunch, Father? Should I keep it warm? It's *cordero asado*."

"No, don't bother. Put it in the refrigerator, Elena. I'll warm it for me and Father Simon when we return."

"*Muy bien*, Father. Tell Father Simon I will be saying a rosary for him."

After hanging up, I sat in the phone booth and thumbed through the Madrid directory until I came to the name *Castro*. There was practically a column of Castros, but only two with the Christian name of Carlos. Neither had the address I remembered from the last time I called. I punched in the number of the first Carlos Castro.

A girl answered the phone. "*Sí, Diga*," she said. There was music and laughter in the background

"May I speak to Carlos Castro, please?"

"Carlos!" the girl shouted above the noise. "Carlos! It's for you."

The next minute a man answered the phone. "Yes, this is Carlos."

The voice belonged to a young man, but I had to be sure.

"Good evening, Señor Castro. I am a friend of Martin Esteban."

"Who?" he shouted into the phone, the music getting louder.

"Martin Esteban."

"You mean Marco Esteban, Jaime's brother?"

I hung up and dialed the second number.

"*Diga!*" The voice was bass, gruff.

"Carlos Castro?" I said.

"*Sí*, this is Carlos Castro. Who is this?" The man coughed from the chest.

"A friend of Martin Esteban."

"What is your name, Señor?" Castro demanded.

I said nothing.

"I said what is your name!"

Satisfied, I replaced the receiver. I wanted to drive to the address listed for Castro. There were so few occasions when I actually had a car and it would be good to take advantage of it now. But I was reluctant to leave Simon at the hospital, even briefly. I returned to the admissions desk and asked the nurse with bleached hair for a status report. She shrugged and pointed to a bearded doctor talking to a man in the waiting room. I waited until he'd finished and approached him about Simon.

The doctor eyed my habit with interest. "He's still being examined, Father. But I believe the ankle is fractured. He's running a fever too, you know."

"Do I have time to do an errand?"

The doctor nodded. "It will be another hour or so, at the least."

I climbed in the Volvo and set out for Castro's neighborhood. His address was not far from the Royal Palace and the Sabatini Gardens, an upper-middle-class area. Castro no doubt owed his place in the upscale neighborhood to jobs like the one he'd performed over 20 years ago.

I wound through narrow streets, shaded from the hot sun, until I reached Pasado del Sabatini, a wide avenue lined with modern apartment buildings. The address corresponded to a fairly new high-rise with balconies. I pulled the car over and double-parked. Which apartment belonged to Castro? My gaze moved from one balcony to another. On the upper floors, where the sun beat hard and strong, potted ficuses and palms thrived and bright petunias sprang from baskets and planters. As the balconies descended, foliage grew sparser. I couldn't imagine Castro cultivating a garden. I couldn't even imagine him living in such a high-class respectable building. I studied the place for five minutes before starting up the engine again.

· · ·

The next week, Santo Domingo held its August retreat—which meant three days of confinement. I'd rather have been at Santiago, waiting hand and foot on Simon, who, it turned out, had broken his ankle. We spent two hours everyday in Eucharistic adoration, on our knees before the white wafer displayed in a monstrance of gold on the altar. And then there was another hour of listening to the retreat master's exhortations from the pulpit. All normal duties of the monks outside the monastery were suspended. It was impossible to get away to Madrid during the day, the only time to catch a glimpse of Castro. My only consolation was Bernardo's arms at night.

One night thunder shook my cell window. He lay next to me, his hands behind his head. The day's sultry heat lingered, and the sheet lay wadded at the bottom of the bed. We'd been talking about the retreat, the hours spent in chapel.

"What do you think about, kneeling there?" I said. I stroked his chest. It was smooth and cool as a stone in a Pyrennean stream.

"I don't know. Mostly I let my thoughts drift."

"Brother Domingo's warnings must have slipped your mind." Domingo had instructed us as novices.

"The dangers of distraction? Maybe. But I think of prayer as sitting in God's company."

"Spoken like a true mystic." I pinched his nipple and he flinched. "You'd never ditch God, would you?"

"Never."

"What about God ditching you? Think he ever would?"

"Never."

"The thought must have crossed your mind. What about when you found out you liked boys?"

"I shut out the feelings, mostly. I loved seminary too much to lose it."

I laughed. "You loved it because you were surrounded by pretty boys."

Bernardo shook his head. "I just loved it. The rhythm of the day—prayer, study, recreation. And the priests cared about us. Father Miguel was my favorite. He taught history. He's the one who got me interested in it. He was very organized. Outlined his lectures on the blackboard. Kept his handwritten notes in a loose-leaf binder, a tab for every century. He made me revise my paper on Lenin three times until I got it right."

"And then gave you a big, fat A-plus, I bet."

"An A-minus."

"*Verdad*? I'm surprised you didn't jump off the roof."

"What do you mean?"

"I mean you're a bit of a perfectionist, *que no*? Oh, don't be offended. It's charming." I patted his cheek when he turned his head away.

"Everything seemed possible there," he said thoughtfully after a moment or two. "Even for boys that...didn't fit the machismo mold."

"The sissies, you mean."

He went on as though he hadn't heard me. "I was soccer captain. I had the leading roles in the annual play." He chuckled. "I once played Ophelia in a condensed version of *Hamlet*." He crossed his hands over his chest and recited in a lyric voice pitched a tone or two above his own. "O what a noble mind is here o'erthrown! The courtier's, soldier's, scholar's eye, tongue, sword. The expectancy and rose of the fair state. The glass of fashion and the mould of form. The observed of all observers—quite, quite down. And I, of ladies most deject and wretched."

I laughed at the thought of Bernardo's heart-shaped face framed by a flowing wig. "I guess if Shakespeare's actors could get away with it, you could too."

"That's what Father Alvarez told us. Our drama teacher. I think he envied me, to tell you the truth."

"He probably wasn't alone." A third of the priests I'd known were repressed drag queens who lived to parade around the altar in silky gold vestments.

A flash of lightning lit the room. Thunder boomed and then came the rain. I went to the window and stuck out my hand to feel the big drops. "I suppose you made valedictorian."

"In a class of 10." He propped himself on his elbows.

"What sage advice did you give your comrades at commencement?"

"None. I just told the old class stories. The day Ricardo got locked in the biology lab, our class trip to Pamplona."

"Don't tell me they let you run with the bulls?"

"No, but one of my classmates climbed under the ropes and joined the runners. José Navarro. A scrawny little kid from Barcelona. Almost got trampled to death. *Pobrecito.* He wasn't really right in the head."

"You did like it there," I said, crawling back into bed.

"Why are you so surprised?"

"I don't know. I guess I can't imagine voluntarily giving up my family."

"Do you think..." He hesitated. "Maybe you idealize them."

"Naturally. What else can I do? I used to imagine what it would have been like—taking vacations together, Christmas holidays, attending a bullfight with my father. He promised to take me to one, when I got older. I remember the moment perfectly. My father was shaving, glancing at me in the bathroom mirror as I described a bullfight I'd just seen on television. He said, 'We'll go, *niño*, when you're 10. That's how old I was when my father took me.' I told him that was years and years away. He smiled and said it would go more quickly than I could imagine. He spoke the truth."

Bernardo reflected a moment. "They say if you're taken from your family at an early age, you never really separate from them."

"They?"

"Psychologists. They say the normal parts of growing up

don't happen. Rebelling. Compromising. Living as an adult in the same town as your parents. No more romanticizing. No more bending over backward to please them."

I nodded. "They're probably right." As I lay there, my eyes shut tight, my insides seemed to empty out like water from a stone fountain, leaving it cracked and dry and baking in the sun.

• • •

Unlike Bernardo, I spent the hours before the altar with a clear focus: the plans that once had been too distant to imagine in any detail. *Murder—what would that be like?* I'd gotten into fights at the orphanage with the other boys. I'd punched a few faces and twisted a few arms. But I'd never plunged a knife into flesh. What would it feel like? What would it feel like to stab Esteban? For all his exercise equipment, his body was soft and flabby. Would the blade sink into his stomach as if it were a ball of bread dough? Or would it meet resistance? Even flaccid muscle tissue had to be ripped. Maybe tearing his flesh would be like cutting through raw chicken.

I focused on the stomach because it was such a vulnerable section of the body. If I began there, Esteban and the others would find their agony prolonged. A quick kill would mean hitting the heart. How hard would I need to stab to get to the heart? Did a sharp knife break through bone easily? If the first blow failed, would the second succeed? The throat might be a better choice for the fatal plunge. Only soft tissue protected the jugular. Slashing a throat must be a grotesque thing. In horror films slashed throats gaped like second mouths. Blood gushed from a severed throat like a fountain.

Blood raised other questions. This red liquid, warm as bath water—would it shoot from the body or flow? Would it seem oddly natural against my own skin, this fluid warm as cum? The practical concerns raised by blood occurred to me too. Should I wear my habit when I killed? It could facilitate access and allay suspicion, but it could also draw attention, especially if covered in blood.

The questions might be moot in terms of Esteban. Of course, I'd do the deed if I couldn't get Bernardo to act. Always a possibility. But if Bernardo thought I was in danger, if he thought his father was on to me and eager to take me out, it wouldn't be so hard to make him kill. And whatever fucked up feelings for Bernardo clogged my thinking— I'd squelch them. That's the way it had to be. If Bernardo killed his father, the weapon made no difference to me. Why should it? My pleasure would come on the front end, in scaring Esteban, forcing him to watch his back until he was striking out at straw targets.

On the Monday after the retreat, I boarded the train for Madrid after mass at Santiago. At Atocha Station I transferred to the city subway and rode to the stop closest to Castro's address. Road construction near the station stirred up dust and caused a traffic jam at the nearby intersection. I walked down the busy avenue and escaped into a shady alley that took me all the way to Castro's street. The doorman at Castro's building noted the habit and nodded respectfully, opening the door for me. I crossed the marble floor of the lobby to the front desk.

"I'm looking for Carlos Castro's apartment," I said to the clerk.

"Certainly, Father." The thin man, in coat and tie, picked up the phone.

"No, please. I would like to surprise him. I'm an old friend."

The man smiled. "Number 841," he said and motioned to the elevator.

My heart thudded as the elevator slowly rose to the eighth floor. If this was the man who'd killed my mother, then it would be the first time I'd laid eyes on him since the day of the murder.

The corridor on the eighth floor was carpeted and illuminated by bulbs glowing in seashell shaped sconces along the walls.

Number 841 was a corner apartment. I rang the bell.

"I'll get it. I'll get it." The voice from inside belonged to a child.

"Wait, Miranda!" a woman called. "Don't open the door without looking."

I smiled at the peephole. The door opened and just over the chain an old woman stared up at me. She seemed pleasantly surprised when she saw the habit.

"Yes, Padre?" she said.

"It's a priest, *Abuelo!*" The little girl shouted from behind the woman.

"*Buenos Días*, Señora," I said. "I'm making visits in the neighborhood. I'm a Salesian. We're helping out at the cathedral during the summer."

"One moment, Padre." The woman closed the door to remove the chain and opened it again. "Please, come in." She stepped aside.

"*Hola*, Padre!" The little girl smiled brightly. She was

fair and chubby with straight black hair that fell to her shoulders. She must have been 6 or 7.

"*Hola.*" I managed a smile. I hadn't anticipated a child in the life of Castro, nor even a wife, if that's who the old woman was. The domestic setting was all wrong.

The old woman led me through the foyer, past several doors, to a large sitting room. She crept along arthritically. Her dull gray hair was pulled into a knot at the nape of her neck. She wore a cotton housedress and slippers. The girl skipped along beside me.

"Carlos," the woman said, "we have a visitor."

When she moved aside, gesturing to a sofa, an old man looked my way. It was definitely the man I'd last seen in my parents' bedroom, pinning down my mother. Twenty years had left his hair sparse and gray and he wore glasses now, but it was the same ugly mastiff face. He wore a short-sleeved shirt. And on his arm, now soft and flabby, a blue cobra lifted its hooded head. For a moment I thought I might pounce on him then and there, in the sight of his wife and granddaughter, without giving a fuck about the conse-quences, even without a knife. I thought I could strangle him easily, this man glaring at me, the last face my mother had seen before having the life ripped out of her. But I breathed in deeply and nodded my head.

"Hello, Señor. I'm Padre José. Just making rounds in the neighborhood." There probably was no need to lie about the name, but I couldn't be too careful.

"Rounds? What for? I don't go to church."

"Carlos, he's a priest," the old woman pleaded.

He glared at her, but seemed resigned to having me there. "I make my first communion this year, Padre." The chubby little girl lifted her leg behind her by the ankle as she gazed excitedly at me.

"That's wonderful."

"Sit down, now, Miranda, and behave yourself." The old woman tapped the girl's foot to get her to stop fidgeting and sit down, which she did, on the sofa near the old man. "Please, Padre, have a seat. Would you like something to drink? Maybe a glass of wine?"

"For God's sake, Maria," Castro barked. "It's 10 o'clock in the morning."

"Maybe some water," I said, sitting in an armchair opposite Castro.

The apartment was light and airy with large glass doors that opened onto a balcony. Plants crowded the tables in the large sitting room and in the dining room, visible through an archway. Simple cotton rugs were strewn here and there on the tile floor, which gleamed. The old woman brought me a glass of water and hovered over me.

"Thank you, Señora."

I sipped from the glass and set in on a glass tabletop, next to a philodendron. Finally she sat in a ladder-back chair.

"According to the directory downstairs, you are the Castro family, right?"

"Yes, Padre," the old woman said. "Excuse my bad manners for not introducing ourselves."

"I'm Miranda," the little girl sang out. "Miranda Maria Diego y Castro." She huddled affectionately against Castro, who had picked up a newspaper and was holding it close to his face to read it.

"What a nice name." I nodded to her and eyed her grandfather. The bastard didn't deserve a doting granddaughter.

"You say you're assisting at the cathedral, Padre?" Señora Castro said. "What a privilege to be in such a beautiful church. I walk there to mass everyday."

"I haven't seen you." I said it before she could.

"We go to the early mass," Miranda blurted. "Six o'clock in the morning. After I make my first communion, I'll get to go up to the rail with Grandmama. Right, *Abuelo*?"

The old man patted her hand.

"Do you go with them, Señor?" I said.

"Why should I?" Castro glanced up from his paper. "The priests just want my money. To hell with them all."

"*Santa Maria*," the old woman mumbled, crossing herself. "Forgive him, Padre. He's not feeling well."

"I'm sorry to hear that, Señor. Is there anything I can bring you?"

The old man grunted something indistinguishable.

With Miranda interjecting details here and there, the old woman prattled on for 15 minutes about her poor widowed son, who had left the girl with them while he worked abroad. The moment she offered to get photographs, I stood up.

"I'm afraid I have to continue my rounds, Señora. Perhaps another time."

She got to her feet as quickly as her arthritic limbs allowed her. "Of course, Padre."

She led me to the door. Miranda clutched my hand along the way.

"Please do come back, Padre. Señor Castro doesn't mean to be so gruff." The old woman gazed earnestly at me as she stood before the door. Her soft, fleshy face was deeply lined.

"I will, Señora. *Adiós*, Miranda." I squeezed the little girl's hand, which clearly delighted her.

"*Adiós*, Padre."

At the request of the old woman, I blessed her and the girl before leaving.

Downstairs, the thin desk clerk nodded to me as I exited the elevator.

"How are the Castros, Padre?"

"Very well," I said, wishing that I'd found the old man in the solitary misery he deserved instead of surrounded by a worshipful family.

That evening Bernardo had overnight duty at San Servando, so I jabbered with a couple of the monks during the recreation period, then paced in my cell until I got drowsy and went to bed. All night strange dreams hounded me—a series of macabre *tableaux vivants*, carefully arranged as if they were being photographed for some sadistic magazine. In one scene, Castro's body lay on a white beach, brilliant houses rising along the cliffs in the background. Blood streamed from the old man's chest, dyeing the sand around him red. Oblivious to the corpse, Castro's chubby granddaughter sat nearby in a scarlet bathing suit, inspecting a sand castle. Another tableau was set in a cemetery. It displayed two corpses, side-by-side, in open coffins, surrounded by mourners. I watched the scene from above. Old Señora Castro was placing a rose on the breast of my mother's corpse. My mother was beautiful, her face clear and glimmering, her dark, luxurious tresses falling over her shoulders. Her dress was white, with a collar of lace. The rose on it was like a wound. In the coffin next to her the nude body of Castro was slashed from head to toe, and blood gushed from all the wounds. A crow pecked away at his shriveled balls. I woke up spooked. More than anything I wanted to climb into Bernardo's bed.

Twelve
BERNARDO

"Why cheat?" I said to José. I stood at my desk with my arms crossed.

"I don't understand this stuff." The gangly boy held his ground, glaring at me resentfully. "I thought history was supposed to be facts and dates, not essays."

"Facts? What are the facts about the Civil War, according to the Republicans? Did it end successfully? Did they benefit?"

"Who cares?" José sneered. "The war ended before I was born."

"Fine, José," I said. "Maybe you'll like Cervantes better. He's timeless."

I sat him down at his desk and opened the book in front of him. He would frown at a line, then transfer everything to his notebook, careful never to glance up or show any awareness of me. It was an old-fashioned exercise, and I hoped it wouldn't ruin Cervantes for him. The passage was from the windmill scene. Most of the boys liked it.

Cheating was a common thing at San Servando. The boys had no qualms about it whatsoever. So many of them had been abused or abandoned, it never dawned on them that something so trivial as copying from someone else's paper could involve morality. Maybe they were right. That's what Juan Ramón would say. But they had to get along in the world outside the walls of San Servando.

When I'd finished grading a half-dozen exams, I sent José away. I took a piece of folded stationary from my backpack and read the bold handwriting, a blockish mixture of printing and cursive script:

Upon my flowering breast
Which I kept wholly for Him alone,
There He lay sleeping,
And I caressing Him
There in the breeze from the fanning cedars.

When the breeze blew from the turret
Parting his hair,
He wounded my neck
With his gentle hand,
Suspending all my senses.

The words from San Juan's *Dark Night* were never so tender—because Juan Ramón had sent them.

During novitiate just the opposite had happened. I'd

done the pursuing—of a swarthy Basque boy.

Yesterday Juan Ramón had grinned when I mentioned the affair. "*Verdad?* A Basque? You know what they say about the Basque men." He tapped his crotch.

We were jogging outside the city walls, along the road overlooking the river. A rim of sun glowed to the west just above San Servando's crenellated tower.

"In his case they were right," I said.

Juan Ramón shot me a glance to see if I was serious.

I nodded emphatically.

"Don't keep me in suspense."

"Let's just say God was good to him."

Juan Ramón snorted. "You mean good to you." He pressed a finger against one nostril, turned his head, and blew his nose. "Well, go on."

"*Entonces*, we were roommates. One night he let me massage his neck and back. And I got carried away." I couldn't bring myself to give all the details about how insistent I'd been with Pedro, reaching lower and lower until I sensed his permission to touch more, his solid thighs, his warm hard member.

"Desperate, huh?"

"I suppose so. But it was more than lust."

"You fell in love."

"Yes," I mumbled, suddenly choked up. It was the first time I'd ever heard those words applied to me. I looked down to the Ponte Nuevo as we passed it. The bridge lay in shadow, quiet and sepia. "But Pedro just tolerated me."

"He never climbed into *your* bed. Is that what you're saying?"

"And he never acknowledged anything between us. I talked to him about everything, my family, exams, God. He treated it like prattle. I finally told him what I felt for him. I didn't use the word *love*. I don't think I could have. I compared us to David and Jonathan."

"And?" Juan Ramón wiped the sweat from his face with the back of his hand.

"The next night he was in a new cell. I couldn't eat or sleep for days. I even thought of killing myself. Except it was a mortal sin." I smiled at the incongruity. "That's what saved me."

"What do you mean?"

"Guilt. Much better than despair. There's a solution for it. Remorse and confession."

"And a firm resolution to avoid the nearer occasion of sin."

We both laughed at the words he'd parroted from the Act of Contrition.

Still, I wasn't sure how much I'd changed since the days of Pedro. I still felt guilty. And what if I should? To commit "impure" acts, violate your vows, wasn't that a heinous sin. Even for love? After all, the illicit love of Dante's Paolo and Francesca had doomed them to flit around the second circle of hell for all eternity, like pathetic doves lost in a storm.

We had jogged quietly for a few moments. Our footfalls on the graveled shoulder landed rhythmically, together.

"I never fell in love," Juan Ramón suddenly said, ruefully. "I was too guarded. Too mean, I suppose."

"*Verdad?*" A wave of panic passed through me. Was he speaking only about the past?

"I'm not saying I didn't fool around. I've already told you that."

"A lot?" I said.

"Enough. Their faces are a blur."

"No one recently?"

He coughed and spit toward the road. "No one special."

His reserve hurt me. He seemed to sense it.

"You're the only man I've ever loved, Bernardo," he said. "That's the truth. It's all that matters. Why waste time describing meaningless trysts?"

In that moment, a wave rushed up inside of me, calming my fears. My love was returned and I was too full for guilt. Soul and body, body and soul, Juan Ramón made them one.

That night, last night, he'd slid into my bed and I had the same feeling. His body next to mine seemed like the most natural thing in the world, like the tide lapping at my feet on the hot shore of Cádiz. His hands over my chest and back, arms and legs were like those of the healing therapists I'd read about, people who could detect pockets of pain or stress or longing. His hands searched my throat and chest and thighs and the soles of my feet, alert to the points of tension or pleasure. Then he applied his bearded lips. He pressed his face against my belly and the small of my back. And when he took his own pleasure, thrusting harder and deeper, his desire excited me and I exploded like a hot fountain.

Afterward I rested against him, now under his arm, now my head against his musky chest.

He brought up the subject of his parents.

"There's more for you to know about their deaths," he whispered. In the faint light from the plaza below, his dark chest hair lay like a shadow on his glimmering brown body.

I waited for more, but he didn't say anything for several moments. I thought he'd drifted back to sleep. Then his chest began to heave in spasms beneath my cheek. I lifted my head and reached to feel the tears on his face.

"I was there, Bernardo," he said. "When they were killed."

"But you said…"

"I was there. There were three men. One had my father pinned down on the bed and another one had my mother on the floor."

I raised myself on my elbow. My heart thumped in my throat.

"The third man held me. He wanted me to see it all. I fought him like hell trying to get to my mother. She was maybe two meters away from me. Say, from here to the door. And you know, she begged the man to take me out of the room. The man on top of her had started taking down his pants."

"You saw him rape her?"

"I passed out. When the man on my father fired his gun. I was sprayed with his blood."

My impulse was to ask about the police or the killers' motives or about why and how the men let Juan Ramón go, anything but rest quietly on his final words. But I forced myself to keep my mouth closed. I succeeded, even when Juan Ramón finally got up without saying more. Then I panicked. *What if he regrets confiding in me?* When he'd gone, I prayed. *Oh God, bring him back. Bring him back again.*

And then I received the note from him. I could have yelled for joy. I'd found it inside my breviary at matins and had read it over and over, while the others chanted the psalms. On the bottom Juan Ramón had scribbled that he wanted to meet me that night. He'd come to my cell when he got back from Santiago, where he had to spend the evening instructing a couple preparing for marriage. I thought about him all day at school.

During vespers I could hardly contain myself. My eyes wandered to the lined faces next to me in the choir, to the sweeping arches above, and back to the page. The chanting had never seemed so off-key. Vicente, Eduardo, half-blind Pablo—the other monks had never seemed so ancient. And for the first time, the chapel felt as confining as a crypt. The smell of beeswax, incense, and old varnish almost choked me.

Afterward, I undressed and waited in my cell for his knock. From the window I watched the light rain shining on the distant sidewalk. Someone on a bicycle raced past a street lamp. Water sprayed from the tires. I sat down at the desk and reread the passage he'd copied for me. Then I reviewed class notes and read his note again. I paced for a while then read from a novel and paced some more. *He must have returned by now. Why hasn't he knocked on my door?* At half past 11, I grabbed my robe, turned out the light, and walked through the quiet corridors to Juan Ramón's cell.

There was no answer when I knocked. I opened the door and whispered his name. No answer still, but there was movement in the bed.

"Juan Ramón? What's the matter?" I closed the door and crawled into his bed. He was stripped naked, lying face down.

"What is it?"

He shook his head and muttered into the pillow. "I don't know. I'm scared."

"Scared?"

"What if you blow me off? What if the pious shit they've brainwashed you with is too much for you to handle? The odds are against me."

"No!" I laid my cheek against his warm back. His

shoulder blade pressed against my temple.

"Tell me I'm wrong, then!"

My chest tightened. The wings of a frantic, trapped bird beat against my rib cage. "I'll never leave you," I said.

"You're trying to convince yourself."

"No, I mean it." And I did *want* to mean it. Maybe I did mean it. I *would* love him whatever the price I paid in guilt. Maybe I *would* keep letting him take me, no matter the price.

He turned over on his back. When I touched his face, his cheek was wet. "I've never confided in anyone but you," he said, his voice hoarse. "Never. I've never talked to anyone about my parents. It's messing up my mind."

"Maybe you shouldn't talk about them."

"No. I want to. I want to get it all out of me. Once and for all. You don't know what it's like. The fucking hate eats at me sometimes, until I think I'll explode." He grabbed my hand. "I want to take you to the apartment building where we lived. Where it happened." He kissed my hand. "I've never been back there."

• • •

Later that week we crossed the Alcántara Bridge on our way to the train station. Juan Ramón had been keyed up since he'd decided to take me to his parent's building. He walked so fast I could barely keep up with him.

While we waited for the train, we stood at the counter of a coffee bar, eating sugared *churros*. We'd been talking about the retreat scheduled before my ordination in the spring. I'd just received information on it from the monastery in Salamanca.

"So you'll go to Salamanca for the retreat?" Juan Ramón dipped a *churro* into his coffee. His face was brown from a summer of sun. He seemed more relaxed now after a mile of exercise.

"Yes, since there are five other candidates. Santa Trinidad can accommodate us." I wiped my lips with a paper napkin. "But my ordination will take place at Santo Domingo, as planned."

"How do you feel about the big day?"

"Excited. Even more excited than I did before my profession. That's a bad bias, I think—to rank ordination higher than entrance into religious life. Still, to be able to consecrate bread and wine, to be able to hear confessions. I can't help it."

Juan Ramón smirked. "You should reserve judgment until your first morning in the confessional, when a line of old women rattle off their peccadilloes like a grocery list."

"You should be happy they only have peccadilloes," I said.

"Why? It would be a bigger thrill to hear one of them confess she'd poisoned her husband's food."

I considered the point for a moment. "Has anyone ever confessed a crime to you?"

"You mean like robbing a bank or committing murder? No, nothing ever that exciting."

"What if someone did commit a crime? How would you convince a penitent to turn himself in to the police?"

"I wouldn't."

I must have looked surprised. Juan Ramón shook his head at me.

"We work for the church, not the state," he explained. "Our obligations are spiritual ones, right?"

"Yes, but a serious crime?"

"It doesn't change anything. God's law is not human law. Human law is too fallible."

When I look back on this conversation, I ask myself how much Juan Ramón actually could predict about what would happen later and what I would go through because of it. At the time, I just thought his comment about fallible human law had to do with his parents' murder.

"Tell me, Bernardo," he said after a moment of silence, "do you think your father will come to the ordination?"

That made me laugh. "The day I throw away my life for good? No, not in a million years."

We walked to the platform and sat on a bench. Only a few people were waiting, a woman with a small child and two or three old men. It was a Saturday and most travelers to Madrid had left early in the morning to take advantage of the entire day.

I brooded for a while about my father but then brightened. "You know, Guillermo plans to bring his whole family to the ordination. Guillermo the gatekeeper. I might as well be his son, he's so proud. Pedro and Anna are coming too. And of course mother will be bringing her whole family."

"What are they like?"

I shrugged. "She's got two older brothers, Manuel and Alfonso. Alfonso's my godfather. When I joined the Salesians he took me out to eat. 'Your last meal,' he said, as if I'd be executed in the morning. I think he was proud, though. He keeps a photo of me taking final vows in his foyer, where everybody can see."

"The kneeling shot, right? Hands folded, eyes raised to the abbot."

I nodded. "My mother told me that Alfonso once

thought about joining the monastery himself. But he was too much of a Romeo. It's hard to imagine. He's probably the ugliest man I've ever seen. He's got beady eyes and a nose the size of a potato."

Juan Ramón laughed. "Maybe he wooed the homely women."

"Maybe. His wife has a bad overbite. My father used to say she could eat an apple through a picket fence."

The humor of the joke appeared to escape Juan Ramón. He glanced down the track. "So, your whole household will be in the front pews on the Feast of Pentecost?" he said.

"It seems that way."

"What a celebration." He slapped my leg.

The train pulled into the station and we climbed in. During the trip, Juan Ramón stared out the window, saying little. He must have been feeling apprehensive. Every now and then he rubbed his palms along the arms of the seat as though trying to wipe something off his skin. I wanted to comfort him, but I thought he'd get impatient with unsolicited assurances.

In Madrid, we transferred to the subway line that went to Plaza de España. We strolled along sidewalks thick with shoppers and Saturday office workers and crossed the busy Gran Via to the Plaza. We stopped at the monument to Cervantes in the square adorned by twisted cypress trees and a reflecting pool. Behind it loomed an elegant 1950s skyscraper.

"That's where we lived, Torre de Madrid." Juan Ramón pointed to the building. "In the penthouse. You can see trees on the terrace."

"What a terrific place for a child," I said, shading my

eyes with my hand as I gazed at the building.

"Yes, it was," Juan Ramón mused. "I used to look out at the city from the terrace and count the yellow taxis. They darted around like little bugs. My nanny used to bring me down here to the Plaza. It seemed like such a long trip, 30 floors down in the elevator, across the busy streets."

"You had a nanny too? Mine was a real sourpuss."

"I don't remember much about her," Juan Ramón said. "She was Portuguese and had a funny accent. Sometimes I made fun of it. It was much better to come down with my father and mother. We used to take walks together, all through the neighborhood. Sometimes we ate at a fancy restaurant—I can't remember the name. Everyone there knew my father."

A siren wailed on the Gran Via, growing louder as it approached and then fading as it passed.

"It must be nice to have good memories of your father," I said.

"He always wore a suit. And his collar was like cardboard, there was so much starch in it. I remember snapping it with my finger."

It occurred to me that Juan Ramón had never mentioned how his parents might have felt about having a monk for a son. When I asked him, he seemed taken aback by the question, as though he had never thought of it himself.

"I mean, they must have been religious people," I said.

"I suppose they were. Not fanatics, of course."

What did that mean? Did he think my mother was a fanatic? Or maybe that I was one? But maybe I was being overly sensitive. "No," I said. "I can't imagine you'd come from a family of pious prigs."

He gazed at me intently for a moment, and then looked up toward the building. "My mother stopped going to mass when her mother died. That was before I was born. I asked her one Sunday why my father and I went to church without her. She said she had a bad back. It hurt to sit for so long. Later my father told me she'd prayed to God when her mother was sick. When she died, Mother felt that he'd let her down. She had no one else. Her brother and father were killed in a car wreck. The only other relatives were more or less estranged. They lived in Barcelona."

"What about your father's family?"

"A brother and a sister. Both a lot older. In Buenos Aires."

"They didn't want to take you? I mean, when your parents were killed?"

"Apparently not. They didn't even come to the funeral."

The funeral. Juan Ramón had never mentioned it. *Should I ask him about it?* He seemed eager to talk so I did.

"It was at San Isidro. Family friends came. My father's business associates, I suppose. I was only 7. Nothing registered at that point. Not after the shock of it all. Men in suits, women in black dresses, perfume. Some familiar faces. Lots of people patting me on the head, women kissing my cheek. Lots of people chirping 'brave little boy.' It's all a blur. My eyes were fixed on the two caskets, both covered with white palls. I remember wondering why tablecloths were spread over them. Were we going to have a meal on them?" He smiled sadly.

If we hadn't been in public I would have put my arm around him, stroked his cheek. I felt for him, someone so strong and brave, braver than I could ever be. He'd known complete devastation. No wonder he could be so hard, so callous. It was a matter of survival.

"Anyway, my mother stopped going to church. She did kneel by me, though, when I said my night prayers."

I couldn't imagine a mother who didn't go to mass. It was usually men who took religion in stride, letting their wives take care of church business. "But your father accepted it."

Juan Ramón shrugged. "He had no choice, I suppose. He was old-fashioned about church. Made me kneel straight during the whole Eucharistic prayer. I wanted to rest my ass on the pew. Made me strike my chest during the elevation of the host. 'It's Jesus,' he told me. 'One day you'll get to receive him in communion.' Of course, he didn't see that day come."

Juan Ramón stroked his goatee and continued to stare at the building.

"No," he suddenly said, "I don't think my parents would want a monk for a son. I think they'd want grand-children."

I grinned. "They wouldn't have them anyway, even if you hadn't entered the monastery."

Juan Ramón shot me an irritated look. "Don't be so sure. Maybe I'd like kids myself."

"Then why did you become a monk?" I fired back.

He looked away and seemed to consider the question. Again it struck me as odd that he had to think about it. Now, of course, I understand why it took him time to formulate an answer. The amazing thing is that what he finally expressed was essentially the truth. I think it was more the truth than he himself knew.

"People need shaking up," he said. "The Church has made them dependent. Children who can't think for themselves. People need to grow up. They need a grown up version of

God too. Not some fairy godfather who grants their wishes if they're good—you know how I feel about that. A fairy godfather who lets them into heaven in the end. They need a God who expects them to make choices, take action. Take risks. Change the goddamned world."

"So you had a mission?"

"Exactly. Much better than a personal, private little vocation, don't you think? Something that makes you open your eyes to the world instead of closing them." He turned and nodded to a bench. "Let's sit down."

"You don't want to walk over and see the lobby of the building?"

He seemed bothered by the idea. He shook his head. "It's remodeled. Everything's different from what I remembered."

When we sat, pigeons fluttered to the pavement to beg for crumbs.

"The day it happened, I'd been at school. They let us out early for some reason. Several of the children lived in my building and a driver picked us up. I remember thinking on the way home that I would take my toy soldiers to the terrace and set up a battle, the reds against the blues. I couldn't wait to get out of the tie and jacket."

I listened quietly. Juan Ramón kept his eyes on the building.

"The doorman, Juan was his name, saluted me in the lobby and I raced my classmates to the elevator. I won and pressed the button to close the doors before they could get in. But my friend David stuck in his hand just before the doors shut and they bounced open again. So we all rode up together. I remember bragging that my apartment was higher than all of theirs. They got off about halfway up, and I rode the rest of the way alone.

"I ran down the corridor to our door and rang the bell. I expected my mother to answer. But no one came. I rang it again and again and started getting impatient. I called for her. The door opened and a strange man was staring me in the face. I said, 'Who are you?' He grabbed me and pulled me into the apartment, but I got away—ran to find my mother. That's when I found her and my father in the bedroom. The two men were holding guns on them. My mother yelled "No!" when she saw me and begged the men to let me go. My father tried to reason with the man holding him and got knocked in the head with a gun for it.

"The man at the door grabbed hold of me. The rest came fast. The first shot made me pass out."

We were both silent. Juan Ramón kicked at the pigeons and they flew away.

"And robbery was the motive, according to the police?" I finally said.

"That's what they said."

"You don't believe it?"

"I don't care why the bastards did it," Juan Ramón said. "They killed both my parents and raped my mother."

"But the police must have come up with suspects?"

"No, Bernardo, they didn't. They didn't lift a finger, even when I described the man I saw at the door."

"But why? Why wouldn't they want to apprehend someone guilty of such atrocious crimes?"

"The Madrid police? Corruption will land them all in hell."

"You're saying the murderer knew important people?"

"Or he was an important man himself. Or maybe my father was not a popular man."

"What was his field?"

"Business. Somewhere. I don't know all the specifics."

For a long time we sat there without talking, the traffic roaring around us. Juan Ramón continued gazing at the Torre.

"Do you pray for them?" I said. "Your parents?"

"You mean for their souls to be freed from purgatory?" Juan Ramón said sardonically. "They went straight to heaven, Bernardo. Their blood absolved them of every wrong they'd ever committed."

"I'm sorry." I touched his leg. "I didn't mean to say they were in purgatory. I just thought it would be natural to pray for them, so you could get healed. Take them with speed, oh God. Embrace them, oh God. Lift them to you! That's what I would want to say."

Juan Ramón turned away from me.

"*Their* pain ended a long time ago," I said. "But yours..."

He glanced back at me, his eyes full of tears. "I pray *to* them, Bernardo! I speak to them, I mean. And I'm not so sure their pain is over. Not as long as the men responsible for their deaths go on living."

"How can you believe that? Everything in our faith goes against it."

He dismissed the remark with a wave of his hand. "Believe whatever you want. I don't have to defend my convictions."

"Your convictions? The justice you want is just revenge to make yourself feel better. It's got nothing to do with the eternal rest of your parents. If you could get the man who killed them, you would rest. At least that's what you think."

"What makes you think it wouldn't appease me? Do you think you know me so well?"

This cut me deeply. "How well I know you isn't the

point," I said. "The point is what Christ teaches. Hate and retribution solve nothing. They're cancer for the soul. They make it grotesque. Christ's way brings wholeness."

"Save your platitudes, Bernardo. Listen to me. Are you listening to me or not?"

I nodded. Suddenly I wanted to kiss him.

Juan Ramón clasped my arm and drew me close to him. His pupils were like pinpoints in the bright sun. "Justice," he said "revenge—call it what you want—it's not futile. You can't tell me that Christ didn't believe in it, either. Woe to you who have your fill now; woe to you who oppress. God wants the scales balanced."

"Then let God do the balancing," I said.

"Why not let God do the forgiving?"

It was stupid of me, trying to reason with him. And self-righteous. I knew it. *Let the mysterious spirit of God blow where it will*, I said to myself. *Into every heart, into every heart.*

"I know their names," he said, calmly now, releasing me and gazing back at the building.

"What?"

"Two of the killers. Castro and Entralgo. I identified them in the police photographs."

"I thought you said…"

"I said the police did nothing. Not then, and not later when I pursued the matter."

"But surely now, as an adult, if you were to get legal help…"

He raised his hand to stop me. "Remember those names. Castro and Entralgo."

Why is he being so mysterious? I wanted to question him further, but I knew it would do no good. He was finished saying what he had to say.

Thirteen
Juan Ramón

At 4 o'clock on a Friday morning, I pulled the knife I'd stolen from the kitchen the night I'd so foolishly gone alone to Esteban's house from the scuffed satchel I'd had since novitiate. The blade was sturdy and sharp enough to strip the fat from a steak with a few quick slices. And the wooden handle was thick and grooved. I could clasp it tight and plunge the blade into flesh without losing my grip. The knife would serve me well.

I wasn't expected at matins on mornings when I said early mass at Santiago. And Simon wasn't expecting me since I'd called in sick the night before. I put on a pair of jeans and a T-shirt, hooking my sunglasses over the collar. I waited until a quarter to 5 when matins started. I grabbed the satchel and left Santo Domingo by the chapel's side door. I had to hustle to make the 5 o'clock train to Madrid, especially since I used meandering side streets to keep away from as many eyes as possible.

Sweating like hell in the warm September air, I reached Castro's apartment building at exactly a quarter to 6. I slipped on the sunglasses and waited across the street at a bus stop. I couldn't risk entering the building until I knew the old woman and little girl had left for church. Within a few minutes, the porter opened the front door and out they walked. The old woman's head was covered with a black mantilla. The little girl's head was bare, her age making her exempt from Church protocol. When they reached the end of the block, I made my move.

Checking to make sure the sidewalk was clear, I crossed the street to a new blue Mercedes parked near the building. Odds were in my favor that the car was equipped with an alarm, and when I jostled it on the driver's side my hunch proved right. The horn sounded quick beats and an alarm wailed. I ducked behind a row of tall hedges that framed the entrance and waited. Just as I'd hoped, the thin, young desk clerk in a jacket and tie dashed out to inspect the car, which probably belonged to a resident. I stepped through a break in the hedges near the door, slipped into the empty lobby, quickly found the door to the stairwell, and climbed the eight flights. Winded, I stopped for a moment on the concrete landing. My T-shirt stuck to my back and the satchel slipped in my wet hand. I set it down and wiped my hands on my jeans. I removed the sunglasses and mopped my forehead with the back of my arm. I picked up the satchel, dropped the sunglasses in, and pulled out the knife. The steel shone in the florescent lighting of the stairwell. The blade would soon rip through the flesh of the pig who raped and murdered my mother.

Outside Castro's door, I slipped the knife into my back pocket, took a deep breath, and rang the bell. After several moments without a response, I rang it again.

"Who is it, damn it?" the old man yelled from inside.

"Padre José," I answered softly, to keep the neighbors from hearing him.

"Who?" the old man cried.

Several seconds passed, probably while he peered through the peephole. Then the door opened. Castro stood there in his pajama bottoms without a shirt. His skin was pasty, his pectorals sagging. The blue cobra was a joke on the arm of the wasting little man, a full head shorter than me.

"It's your granddaughter, Miranda," I said.

Castro looked confused. "What? She's at church."

"I just came from there. Can I come in?"

The old man opened the door, and I stepped in quickly. Before the old man could turn around after closing the door, I dropped the satchel and swung my right arm around his neck, pressing his body against mine. With my free hand, I whipped the knife out of my back pocket and pushed the tip against the soft flesh just under Castro's sternum.

"What is this? What are you doing, goddamn you?"

I turned the old man around and forced him forward and through the first open door off the hallway. The room had an unmade twin bed in it and an American rocking chair full of stuffed animals, apparently the little girl's room. I shoved Castro to the floor and knelt over him, straddling his body and pinning his arms back with my knees. I lowered the knife to his throat.

"Struggle," I said, "and you die, here and now."

The old man's face flushed. His chest heaved under me as he tried to catch his breath. His brown eyes seemed ready to pop out of his face.

"Who the hell are you?" he said, gasping for breath. "What do you want?"

"Shut up." I pushed on the knife until a button of blood appeared on his stubbly throat. "I do the talking. Do you hear me?"

"Yes," Castro whispered.

"I'll tell you who I am. I'm Juan Ramón Fuertes, Señor Castro. Does that name sound familiar?"

The old man stared in terror at me, but with no hint of recognition in his eyes.

"I'm the son of Alicia Fuertes. The woman you raped and killed. In front of me, you bastard, a pleading little boy. Remember?" I pressed the knife into Castro's soft flesh and once again drew blood. "Do you remember?"

"Yes." Castro strained to speak.

"I'm going to give you a choice. Tell me where I can find Entralgo. Tell me, and you live. He's the one I want, not you." I braced myself to finish the lie. "My mother was a whore. You did me a favor. My father is another story. The man who killed him has to pay. So, you want to live?" I raised myself and slammed my body against him.

He winced.

"Where is he?"

"I...I don't know. I haven't seen him since then."

"Don't lie to me, you bastard." I applied pressure to the knife.

"I'm not." Castro struggled for breath now. "I don't know."

The old man had hardly uttered the final word, when I yanked the bedspread from the mattress, drew it over him, repositioned the knife and leaned on it with all my weight. It sank through skin and cartilage and seemed to strike Castro's spine. When his body was completely still, I drew out the knife and uncovered his face. The eyes were open, fixed in terror.

I got up and surveyed the body. It sprawled before me on the bare tile, more like a troll from a children's fable than a man, a troll who'd finally come to his due end.

I bent over the bed and wiped the knife on the blanket. Then I found the bathroom and rinsed the blade clean, until all traces of the blood had disappeared even from the porcelain sink. I wiped the blade with a towel. Then I splashed water on my face and used the towel to dry it. In the mirror I saw that my pupils were dilated and my cheeks flushed. I was looking at a man who had killed. I took a deep breath to calm myself.

I picked up the satchel from the hallway and dropped in the knife. I hadn't been worried about fingerprints in the bathroom. Mine weren't on record anywhere so any prints wouldn't lead to me.

Just as I touched the door handle, I heard the elevator open and the little girl prattling. The mass had lasted less than the 30 minutes I'd counted on, or maybe it had been canceled. I stepped into the girl's bedroom and stood back from the door, shutting it slightly to block their view of the floor. The key turned and the door opened. The little girl shot down the hallway toward the kitchen. The old woman followed her slowly. Through the doorway, I watched her hobble to the kitchen, undoing her mantilla as she walked.

Once the hall was clear, I dashed to the door and turned the bolt as quietly as possible. Inspecting the corridor, I stepped out and pulled the door softly shut. I made it all the way to the fourth floor of the stairwell before I heard the screams. I opened the door on that floor and checked the hallway. Finding it empty, I ran down to the fire exit at the end of the hall. I descended concrete steps, put on my sunglasses, and crossed the parking lot that took me to the other side of the block.

Fourteen

Bernardo

Gracias a Dios! A beautiful cold front had pushed out Toledo's heat in the first week of October. But a sun unfiltered by a single cloud left me as toasted as the dazzling stones of the Plaza de Ayuntamiento. I turned down the mew at the side of the cathedral and entered it through the clock door. The bright daylight gave way to subdued illumination, and the temperature dropped noticeably. But the soaring arches and regal columns of the cold, cavernous building transformed it into the antechamber of heaven. I proceeded to the sacristy. The nun in charge of vestments was supposed to meet me there, rather than in the treasury where my chasuble was stored and where space was tight. Not *my* chasuble, really, but one of the antique vestments owned by the cathedral. Abbot Baroja had arranged for me to borrow one of these chasubles for my ordination ceremony, already being planned though it was over six months away.

Bright lighting in the sacristy sharpened the details of the winged figures on the ceiling. A woman in a floral scarf and a blue coat was giving a tour to a group of tall, Scandinavian-looking people. I approached a nun who was directing a custodian to draw a cart toward her in a corner of the spacious hall. A chasuble lay on the cart.

"Sister Maria Teresa?" I said.

The woman nodded. She was almost as tall as me and solidly built. Her wimple and veil accentuated her large features. Her tranquil gray eyes and her slight smile suggested a certain playfulness. "I think this must be your chasuble, Brother?"

"For an afternoon, anyway."

"Well, let's try it on, shall we?"

The silver-haired custodian helped her lift the chasuble over my head. The stiff red garment hung heavily on me, as though it were soaking wet. It was embroidered with gold thread and fell well below my knees.

"It's beautiful," I said.

"Yes," the nun said, adjusting the chasuble on my shoulders. "It's a 19th-century fiddleback. Recently restored. Our nuns are very proud. You need to tie it behind you, like an apron."

I drew the cords of the front flap of the chasuble behind my back, leaving the back flap hanging free. "Your community maintains the vestments?"

"Now, yes. Some of our older sisters have come down from Madrid to do the work."

I touched the piping. "I can't believe it. Look, I'm shaking." I stretched out my hand to show her.

Sister Maria Teresa smiled and patted my arm. "I thought of this chasuble immediately when Abbot Baroja told me that you would be ordained on Pentecost. The red, I mean, for the season of Pentecost. The sisters who worked on it were thrilled."

"I hope they will come to the ordination. You too, sister."

I wanted to see myself in a mirror but was too embarrassed to ask if there was one in the sacristy. The Scandinavian tourists had noticed me and several of them starting clicking their cameras. The guide ordered them to stop, reminding them that flash photographs were not allowed inside the cathedral. I relished the feel of the vestment on my body for a moment, and then reluctantly untied it and allowed the nun and the worker to lift it over my head.

I walked back to Santo Domingo in a daze. Images of ordination day flashed through my mind. I saw myself prostrate on the stone floor, my arms spread in cruciform, while the monks chanted the litany of the saints. Then I saw Juan Ramón dressing me in the red vestment. Dressing me, then offering me the kiss of peace. One night, lying in the dark on my mattress, he'd promised to be my acolyte.

"It will be like a marriage, won't it," he said.

"Between me and Christ or you and me?"

"Hmm. An interesting question. You'll have to decide."

"What do you mean?" I said. "You want to run off with me to an Alpine retreat?"

"Why do we need to run off anywhere?"

Once again, I hadn't asked Juan Ramón to explain. It was better not to ruin such moments by thinking too much. I could wind up as miserable as I'd been on the day I'd gone to confession at the cathedral. What a difference between this visit and that one! Then, like a drug addict huddled in one of Madrid's urine-ridden backstreets, I was bereft of dignity and hope, and worse, of grace. Today, I was bursting with grace, as big and pure and confident as the Holy Father himself. The weighty scarlet chasuble had embraced me like the love of God. Everything felt possible. My love for Juan Ramón and Christ were not incongruous but one and the same in some mysterious way. The impracticalities of our love, the vows I'd taken—these were unsolved problems, not ghastly judgments.

Fifteen

JUAN RAMÓN

For days after killing Castro I was jumpy. I dropped things. During mass one morning a full paten slipped out of my hands when a window slammed shut in the sacristy. Wafers flew across the floor like white poker chips. I knocked over my glass at dinner on two separate nights. Then, whenever I heard a siren, my heart raced like a motor. And when a strange man in a suit went into Baroja's office one day, I nearly pissed myself thinking it could be a police detective. The dream about Castro laid out on the on the beach woke me several nights. I'd get up and pace for a while, think about going to Bernardo's cell, and then decide against it. Better to hold off until things returned to normal. In fact, I made excuses for staying out of his bed until I couldn't anymore without risking his suspicion. I'd told him Simon was working me to death at Santiago.

It was after 11 o'clock the night I finally knocked on Bernardo's door. I found him grading papers at his desk. Almost two weeks had gone by since Castro.

"How about a break?" I said.

"Sure. Look at this." He handed me a paper with a verse scribbled on it.

"What is it?"

He grinned. "Read it."

I did and smiled. I read the last line aloud. "Franco saved our country's skin, from revolutionary sin." The whole poem was more of the same shit. "You better stick to teaching history, Bernardo. I don't think you'll turn the boys into poets." I handed him the sheet and sat on his bed.

"This wasn't my idea. Miguel said he felt inspired."

"The student who's been giving Tomás such a hard time? He's come around, I guess."

Bernardo gave me a doubtful look. "He's better."

"What about Tomás? Any more attacks?"

"He's calmed down. He's made a friend."

"*Verdad?* That's hard to believe."

Bernardo shrugged. "A new boy. Lonely. Like Tomás. Things have calmed down."

"Guess we can keep our fingers crossed." I lay back on the bed. "*Oye*, I've got something for you."

"What?"

"Turn out the light and come see."

The light vanished. I heard Bernardo removing his habit.

He opened my robe. His tongue tickled my balls. My cock slid into his mouth. He worked it. But nothing happened. I pulled him up to me, kissed him, my tongue deep in his mouth until I got hard. Then, when I knelt to direct his mouth to my cock, it softened again. "It's not going to happen," I whispered. I lay back on the bed.

"*No importa*," he said, turning to kiss my cheek.

"It's fatigue, I guess." This was a first. I have to admit I felt cut down a notch or two. "Simon's had me organizing more records, carrying boxes of them to the basement. Then I'm running around the city, taking documents to the bishop, visiting sick parishioners. I'm dead on my feet. What if I do you?" I reached for his cock. It was hard.

"No." He pushed my hand away. "I can wait."

"Suit yourself." *To hell with him*, I thought. I'd never been turned down before.

"This is enough," he said consolingly. "I could lie next to you like this and be perfectly satisfied."

"Spoken like a true celibate."

Bernardo laughed.

"What's so funny?"

"Can you imagine Eduardo and Vicente in bed together?"

I imagined shriveled, beady-eyed little Eduardo and fat Vicente going at it.

"Not without puking," I said.

"You think any of the others have ever had sex?"

"I think they're all sexless."

"That's what people say about monks, isn't it?"

"A well deserved label."

"But they must have had urges once. I mean the monks at Santo Domingo. How did they cope? How did they compensate? They don't seem miserable. Maybe they've really made their peace with celibacy."

"You're asking the wrong person," I said. I had never wasted time speculating about the sex lives of old monks. And I didn't have to speculate about the young ones—at least not those I'd taken to bed during novitiate.

"Baroja once told me he's always missed having a wife. Someone to talk to at the end of the day. Someone to grow old with, to raise children with."

"What? The monastery hasn't fulfilled his every need?"

"Don't you like Baroja?"

"He's all right, as far as abbots go."

"I like him."

"You like everyone." I knocked my head against his. A sudden sense of regret balled up in my stomach. *What's planned is planned*, I told myself. Then I remembered how good it felt to see Castro dead. That relaxed me.

Sixteen
BERNARDO

Brother Diego's white terrier greeted me in the monastery's entrance hall when I got back from school one day. Diego stepped out of his office. He had sliced an apple on a saucer and now stuck a piece into his mouth.

"Say, you never told me how you liked the chasuble," he said.

"It's beautiful." I scratched the dog behind the ears, then accepted a slice of apple from Diego. "It's a 19th-century fiddleback."

The red-haired monk smiled, rather dull-eyed, maybe unsure of what I meant. He let the dog sniff his saucer when it trotted over to him. "Oh, Father Baroja wants to see you. Your ordination papers came in."

I knocked on Father Baroja's open door. The abbot looked up from his desk and motioned for me to come in.

"Have a seat, Bernardo." He got up, shut the door, and sat down again behind his desk. Several piles of paper were neatly stacked on it around a large, healthy philodendron whose vines trailed to the floor.

I liked the abbot's office, probably the most comfortable room in the monastery. I liked the smell of the books lining the walls, and I liked the pattern of the worn oriental rug covering most of the stone floor. The two armchairs upholstered in brown leather were large and comfortable, and the sturdy oak desk, darkened with age, seemed to anchor the room to the earth. Family photographs, including the school pictures of several children, cluttered the top of the file cabinet behind the abbot's desk. And above it, on the office's one free wall, hung a massive painting of the monastery, in a rococo frame. The painter had sat in the plaza across from the two towers of the chapel, rather than in front of the shadowed facade of the monastery's entrance. In the painting, the tiles of the chapel's roof gleamed in full sunlight, which seemed an extension of the real sunlight streaming in from the office's tall side window.

"Brother Diego says my ordination papers came."

Baroja nodded. "Yes. The bishop likes to have the paperwork done well in advance." He patted the pile of paper nearest him.

He seemed uncomfortable. He scratched his bald forehead a moment, his eyes on the documents but clearly not focused on them.

"Is there a problem with the forms? Are you missing any of my documents?" Prior to ordination the archdiocese had to have records of birth, baptism, confirmation, and, in the case of candidates in religious communities, documentation of temporary and final vows. But perhaps there were other records I knew nothing about.

Baroja stood, came around to my side of the desk, and sat in the other armchair. From such a close distance, he looked tired. His gentle eyes, brown flecked with gold, were puffy and underscored with dark circles. He seemed tense too. Usually he crossed his legs and leaned back in the chair. Today he kept his feet planted solidly on the floor and sat very erect, his large hands with their knobby fingers folded on his lap.

"I'm at a loss for how to begin, Bernardo. Forgive me."

A wave of alarm spread through me. I silently waited for the abbot to proceed.

Baroja took in a deep breath and released it, apparently gaining a sense of determination. "We must talk about your relationship with Juan Ramón. I've put it off for some time, hoping, I suppose, that everything would right itself."

My face suddenly burned. I turned my eyes to the philodendron. The foliage was thick on the side nearest the window. The leaves on the dark side strained toward the light.

"I don't want to play the confessor, Bernardo. It's not my place. But I hope and pray that you have opened yourself to your own spiritual director over these past months. It's essential. If you have then perhaps everything can remain on course."

"On course?" My voice came out a pitch higher than usual.

Baroja nodded. "For ordination."

Oh, dear God, I thought. *Not this. I'm not hearing these words.*

"Have you been in regular contact with your director? It's Father Alphonsus, isn't it? At San Servando."

"Yes."

The old priest said daily mass in San Servando's chapel. I met with him each Thursday afternoon. Our sessions began with a prayer. Then Father Alphonsus lectured about whatever aspect of the holy priesthood came to his mind that day and asked me if I wanted him to hear my confession. He was partially deaf and I'd shamelessly taken advantage of the fact by whispering my sins—including the ones against celibacy. Father Alphonsus rarely asked me to repeat anything, probably assuming my transgressions were what Juan Ramón called peccadilloes. He probably also assumed that since I never broached any concerns I had nothing troubling to confess.

"Of course, as a formality, Father Alphonsus will sign a statement before your ordination, expressing his confidence in you as a candidate." Baroja seemed to wait for me to confirm that Alphonsus would certainly do this.

"Yes, Father. I know."

"Bernardo..." Baroja hesitated, wrinkling his bald brow and studying his foot. "If there is anything in your friendship with Juan Ramón that can't be reconciled with your vow of celibacy, then we are discussing a very serious matter." He looked up at me now. "I'm not speaking morally, not strictly. I'm speaking about a conflict. About a component of yourself that you must address and resolve before ordination."

"Does a monk's every question have to be answered before ordination day?" I said.

"No," Baroja said calmly. "Of course not. But things like this must be confronted. What if you should choose another way of life?"

"I would never do that, Father. *This* is my life. It's everything I have waited for since I was a child. It's everything to me."

He considered my words a moment. "There's something else, Bernardo. I've observed it. I've been concerned."

What else? I thought. *How could this be any worse?*

"I am worried that Juan Ramón might be...pushing you in a direction you're not inclined to take." He raised his hand before I could object. "I don't mean in a malicious way. I only mean that he is a strong-willed man. He has the power to influence, especially someone who is trusting and perhaps somewhat passive by nature."

"Are you saying that I am infatuated with Juan Ramón?" My heart was pounding by now.

Baroja shrugged. "It's something that happens in a monastery among young monks. And it does not necessarily include inappropriate behavior. I'm telling you, Bernardo, your behavior is not my principle concern. It is the disposition of your soul. Its health. My job is not to grow and maintain monks, but to protect their spiritual well-being."

"With all due respect, Father, it sounds like you feel obligated to weed out the bad ones."

"There are no bad ones, Bernardo. You must believe me."

Baroja gazed sympathetically at me.

"What will you do?"

"I don't know. But I must be honest with you. If I don't feel you are ready for ordination, I will withhold my approval."

I squeezed my eyes shut.

"That is the worst possible scenario, Bernardo. You need to know. But much can happen in six months. If you continue speaking to your spiritual director and continue praying, there's no reason the community cannot celebrate your ordination on Pentecost day. I just want you to be truly ready to take this step."

"What about Juan Ramón?" I said, looking at Baroja now. "Have you spoken to him?"

Baroja nodded rather gravely. "Yes, I have."

"You've instructed him to leave me alone?"

"Quite frankly, I spoke to him about transferring to another monastery."

I stared at him in complete shock.

"But San Servando needs him now," Baroja continued. "And I think his absence would make it too easy for you ignore the task at hand. You must confront your feelings."

"This is a test, then."

"Perhaps." Baroja shrugged. "But not of your will power, Bernardo. I certainly think you capable of restricting your time with Juan Ramón for six months. No, the only test will be the one within your soul. You must test your calling to a life of celibacy. And you must know and embrace your nature."

My nature. Despite Baroja's compassion, I couldn't help feeling like some kind of grotesque deviant.

After Baroja dismissed me, I went to the chapel and knelt at the communion rail. My head was spinning. I might never wear the embroidered chasuble. I might never lie prostrate before the altar while the monks chanted the litany. The moment I'd dreamed of from the time I was 12 years old might never happen. And what of Juan Ramón? How could I stand to lose him? Baroja was wrong. What I felt was love, not infatuation. Just the wrong kind of love. How had this happened? How had I let myself jeopardize my ordination? *O Cristo!* I prayed, raising my eyes to the crucifix at the pinnacle of the reredos. *Please make this go away. Please catch me up in your arms. This love is too painful. What is it you are requiring of me? Have I wronged you by loving him?*

That night Christ seemed to answer me in a dream. It was dark as the open *meseta* on a moonless night, but I knew exactly where we were. The slate floor of the chapel was cold and rough against my bare skin. I could feel the high altar towering over us, Christ peeking at us from behind the tabernacle curtain. The smell of incense and candles mixed with the musky smell from Juan Ramón's furry chest. The boldness of the rendezvous place excited me. As Juan Ramón encircled me with his arms, pressed his muscular thighs against me, I felt the familiar sensation, wild and dark, stir in my loins. Suddenly the chapel filled with daylight. The other monks stood in the choir stalls, gazing down at us over open breviaries. Abbot Baroja, in a black chasuble, mounted the steps to the pulpit and raised the thick red lectionary, ready to hurl it at us. The monks chanted a Gregorian *kyrie*. As the tempo hit a frantic speed, a shrill scream echoed against the vault. Up in the rafters, my mother dangled from a rope around her neck. Her shoes dropped, one after the other, onto the slate floor next to my head. I started crying, and when I opened my eyes in my dark cell tears streamed down my face.

• • •

"You mean you want to give me up, Bernardo?" Juan Ramón said. "Just like that?"

"What else can we do?"

"We? I know what I want."

"But how?" I said. "I want to be ordained."

Juan Ramón embraced me. We were standing in the dark mosque of Cristo de la Luz. We'd crept out of Santo Domingo after vespers.

"You *will* be ordained," he whispered. "Do you think Baroja would really stop you? He has no proof of anything."

"He doesn't need proof. Suspicion is enough to make him withhold his approval. He said so."

"He doesn't mean it."

"Oh, God." I pulled away and went to the window. The soft light from street lamps fell on the terra-cotta rooftops. My breath smoked before me in the crisp October air.

"And what if he does, Bernardo?"

"It's my *life*," I said.

Juan Ramón came over to the window. "What about *our* life?"

I shook my head. "In the monastery you mean? Do we just go on sneaking around at night, waiting until we can find some place to hide? How do we know that we'll even stay here together? I could be assigned to a parish in Madrid." I sighed in exasperation. "Why didn't you tell me that Baroja approached you? Why didn't you warn me?"

Juan Ramón shrugged. "He gave me the impression that I was the problem. The warning was for me. I didn't think he'd talk to you."

"All the same..."

"Do you love me, Bernardo?" Juan Ramón clasped my arm.

"Don't!"

"No, tell me!"

"I have told you. You know I do."

"Then where's your faith?"

"Don't make me laugh."

"I wouldn't give *you* up for anything. No matter what."

"You're already ordained," I said. "You can't lose that."

"I would leave it behind if I had to."

I looked at his beautiful matador's face now in shadow, at the silhouette of his strong shoulders, his throat exposed above the wool cape. "You'd leave the monastery?"

He nodded. "With you, yes. If I had to."

What a thought! I'd never disobeyed my superiors. I'd never been tempted to. Obedience had always been in my favor, like commands to a child to eat his vegetables or to look both ways before crossing a street. This was the first time I'd ever questioned anything. I wasn't even sure what Baroja was asking of me. How did I come to terms with sexuality? By accepting it? If so, then what? Control it the way diabetics control the production of insulin in their bodies? Or destroy it altogether like a dangerous infection? Surely Baroja could not mean to accept such a predisposition by cultivating it, like some kind of latent talent. I doubted whether Baroja or any authority in the Church would admit the implications of San Juan's words. *Upon my flowering breast which I kept wholly for Him alone, there He lay sleeping, and I caressing Him... He wounded my neck with his gentle hand, suspending my senses.* Such images are drawn from real experiences, or they mean nothing! Besides, *sexuality* meant nothing to me in that moment. I loved Juan Ramón. The reality of my predicament was that simple. In that moment, I thought I could very possibly leave the monastery behind to follow him.

"We could go to Barcelona or Valencia," Juan Ramón told me. "We could even go to Buenos Aires if we wanted."

He said that in certain cosmopolitan circles there having *maricons* as friends improved a person's status. Not that Juan Ramón used the word *maricon*. He compared us to Achilles and Patroclus, classical heroes. Maybe we had a radical vocation, he argued. Didn't God circumvent, even confuse conventional measures of goodness? Christ had favored the dregs of society. Gustavo Gutiérrez, a theologian we'd studied, described Christ's favor as a preferential option for the oppressed. The very ones society and religious institutions scorn, they are the favored ones. And the true Christian sacrifice? Surrendering the esteem of society and Church.

I listened to him in a daze. I didn't know anything any more. Then he stopped.

"There's something I want to show you," he said. He pulled a piece of paper from his pocket and gave it to me. "Read it."

I held the paper up in the scant light. It was an article torn from the newspaper. The headline said "Man Killed in San Isidro Neighborhood."

"What is this?" I said.

"It's from today's paper. Read it."

I scanned the brief article:

> Carlos Olvides Castro, age 67, was found stabbed to death in his apartment two blocks from San Isidro Cathedral. No suspects have been apprehended in the case, according to Inspector Alphonsus Duran of the Madrid Department of Police.

"I don't understand," I said.

"Look at the name."

I remembered now. Castro was one of the men who'd murdered his parents. A chill ran up my spine. "What does it mean?"

Juan Ramón raised his hand to hold off my question. He slipped another piece of paper from his pocket. "Now read this."

The folded page turned out to be a letter, typed on a manual typewriter and full of typographical errors.

My dearest son,

It's time I confessed to you. I deserved to die. The world was a better place after I was killed. You will join me here soon. Hell is a lonely place, so I look forward to seeing you. The flames torture but never consume. The charred odor is the worst thing. Black, charred flesh. The bad ones burn, Juan Ramón. You will join me, just like your mother. Just like the others. A habit won't save you.

Your loving Papa

There was no signature and nothing written on the back of the page.

"This is sick," I said.

"Not as sick as the last one." Juan Ramón took the letter from me, folded it, and stuck it back in his pocket. "From my mother. She confessed she was a whore who deserved what she got. This letter makes four. When they first started, I thought some demented idiot had gotten information about my past and decided to shake me up. Then the letters included certain details—my mother on the floor, my father on the bed. I figured it was one of the killers, out to finish the job."

"You mean kill you? But why, after all these years?"

"I don't know. I've just been waiting to hear something about Castro or Entralgo. And now I have."

"But why would one of them want to kill the other?"

Juan Ramón shrugged. "Insanity? How the hell do I know?"

"Have you told Baroja?"

"Why? What could he do?"

"Then you should go to the police."

"I have. When I took Simon to the hospital. They said they would look into it. I suppose now they'll take me seriously."

"And find the other man?"

"Entralgo? Yes, I suppose."

"That's a relief."

"It would be, if they were competent. But I guess they're better than nothing."

I stroked his cheek. It was rough. He must not have shaved that day.

He pulled me to him and kissed me, first tenderly, then with heat, pushing his tongue into my mouth, pressing his groin against mine.

Dizziness came as his solid body pressed me against the stone wall. Then he knelt and lifted my habit. For the first time he took me in his warm mouth. My fingers raked his thick, coarse hair. *And I, caressing him...caressing him...*

His motion urged me. He demanded.

Panting like a runner approaching the finish line, I filled him with my seed. With my very self.

Seventeen
Juan Ramón

A week of rain left me restless. Cooped up at Santiago and Santo Domingo, I had to go somewhere, do something different. When the skies cleared on Sunday morning I decided to go to Madrid, but not to Esteban's, despite the magnetic force pulling me there. *Let it all happen*, I told myself. *It's all set into motion. Let it happen.* Now was the time to gather myself at a safe distance. No excuses had to be offered to Bernardo. Watchdog Baroja made communication dangerous.

"He's impressionable, Juan Ramón," Baroja had said to me. "Admiration becomes infatuation. He'll be guilt-ridden. And there's no need. Spare him. Think of his ordination."

Spare *him*, Esteban's son? Spare *him*, goddamn it? But was I swearing at Baroja or myself? *No*, I told myself. *Shake off the sweet dreams. To hell with Bernardo. I needed him for one damn thing—perfect, beautiful symmetry.* It had become a matter of honor, some sort of pledge to my father. Ruin one more son. Fuck him up good. Then the chaos could sift down into God's pure world.

I went to the Toledo train station directly from Santiago. I'd said mass and eaten the noon meal with Simon. The old man's condition was getting more pathetic by the day. I had to dress him for mass. He stood there like a docile toddler being readied for school. The housekeeper had twice found him on the floor in his bedroom and called me at the monastery to come lift him. Simon could have gone to the nursing home run by the diocese if he would only give up his delusions about getting better. But he wouldn't. "*Mira*," he'd said to me one morning, "I can walk without the cane." Then he took a few steps, concentrating like a drunk trying to prove his sobriety.

In Madrid I took the subway as far as the station nearest the Teatro Real and from there boarded a bus that went to a quiet neighborhood full of tall pines and cypresses. I walked past a block of stately mansions inhabited by Madrid's old families. My paternal grandparents had lived in one of them. My father had walked with me there and pointed out the house when I was 5 or 6. Now I couldn't remember which of the stone and stucco structures it was. At the end of the street a wrought-iron gate opened to a cemetery. I entered and followed the familiar gravel path to a section marked by a stone sculpture of the crucified Christ with the Virgin and San Juan standing at his feet. The headstone of my parents rose from the ground two meters from the statue, and now lay beneath its shadow. Creeping juniper blanketed the grave, and a vase of withered chrysanthemums rested at the head. I'd brought them two weeks before. I pitched them out and knelt. The earth, softened by the recent rains, sank beneath my knees.

The inscription on the granite might have been engraved yesterday instead of over 20 years ago. The letters were deep and clean. *La Familia de Fuertes y Corona, Ramón Alphonsus y su esposa Alicia Isabel Duarte. Con los ángeles.* With the angels. Miraculously, someone in authority had solicited and obeyed the wishes of a 7-year-old boy. The phrase had come to me instantly: with the angels. With the angels and with each other, and Juan Ramón alone. *Que lastima, que no?* These were the cards dealt to me.

But I had my own cards to play, did I not? If Trojan Hector could fight despite his destiny, so could I. This resolution had formed in me in a lecture hall long ago, when the classics teacher, his heavy jaws moving machine-like, bellowed out Hector's vow: *To stand up bravely, always to fight in the front ranks of Trojan soldiers, winning my father great glory, glory for myself.* If only Hector's fate had not been inverted for me. Old Priam survived to see his son's corpse pierced through the heels and dragged. The tragedy belonged to the father, not to the son. My wish was selfish as hell. But it had never dissolved.

I thought of a new strange dream I'd had about my mother. She stood on the hot shore, looking out to the sea, her dress rippling in the breeze. I sat on a rock behind her and watched a dark man approach her, his pant-legs rolled up, his white shirt unbuttoned and flapping like the wings of a desperate bird.

"Mama, watch out!" I called in a little boy's voice.

She reeled around, saw the man, and laughed at me. The man turned and laughed too. It was Esteban. A forest of black hair covered his chest. My mother raced to him and ran her hand through the hair.

"No!" I cried. I stood on the rock, making fists at my sides.

Behind them, the rhythmic tide suddenly swelled into a massive, frothing wall that broke over their bodies and pulled them into itself. When it receded, the beach was empty.

• • •

That night I was called to the bed of a dying parishioner. I'd anointed her and read the right prayers over her and wanted to get out of the room reeking of piss and crowded with relatives. I'd carried out my duty and there was nothing more I could do for these people. Who knew how long the old woman would hold on? She could last until morning. But they all expected me to stay. I knew, of course, that if Simon were there, he would stay until the bitter end. So I took a seat near the bed and the people started up the rosary again. I hadn't brought a rosary, and after a moment or two, a little boy offered me his and I took it, fingering the beads as the prayer progressed. After two more rosaries, parents began taking children home and people who'd been kneeling sat down to rest. A few stalwart souls stayed on their knees, including a nun who took care of the big, clumsy daughter who was mentally retarded. I started to doze and the next thing I knew, there was a commotion around the bed and the other daughter was calling me.

Rodríguez, the husband, was leaning over his wife, clutching her hand, looking stunned, as though she'd only had a sinus infection, not cancer, and this could not be happening. The retarded daughter was whining now and swiping at the nun who tried to calm her. The other daughter looked at me through swollen, bloodshot eyes—pleading. With my thumb, I traced the sign of the cross on Señora Rodríguez's forehead. Her face was already jaundiced, sunken—her skull looked like it would cut through her skin. She took a breath, exhaled, and didn't breathe again.

I drew the daughter's husband aside, a tall, sober looking man in a white oxford shirt who'd stepped back when the hysteria began. After we discussed funeral plans, he led me down the stairs and unlocked the front door of the shop beneath the apartment to let me out.

The night was still warm. I had to escape the close, narrow streets where the cloying scent of the apartment seemed to linger. I crossed the Plaza del Ayuntamiento. The dark cathedral rose like a hulk abandoned at sea on a moonless night. I turned toward the lights of Calle Comercio and followed the avenue to Plaza de Zocodover. The outdoor cafés were still full of people. There was only one thing I wanted, though, and I wasn't sure exactly why. It wasn't from some urge to terrify or even harass, though I probably wasn't adverse to that. It was more like a desire for some kind of connection no matter how perverse.

I stepped inside a small café and asked the cashier for change. The short, curly-haired man seemed surprised to see a monk at midnight but gave me the *pesetas* without comment. The tables were occupied by young couples and packs of friends who probably met there routinely. *Some day*, I thought, *this kind of life will be mine.*

In the *interurbano* phone booth, I pulled out a scrap of paper from my pocket. I'd scribbled the number on it. I punched the buttons and waited. The phone rang a dozen times before someone picked up.

"*Diga*," she said, faintly. It was the old woman, Castro's wife. When I didn't speak she said, "Who is this? Who do you want?"

What did I want to say? He got what he deserved? Don't waste your tears on him? I'm sorry for you? I didn't know.

She repeated her questions twice more before hanging up.

I hung up, but didn't put down the receiver. I'd noticed the pretty waiter I'd seen on my first day in Toledo. He was sitting alone at a table near the window. He hadn't seen me. To watch him more easily, I pretended to continue with the phone call. He wore jeans and a silky *maricon* shirt the color of the purplish caladiums in the shady part of the monastery courtyard. He sat slightly slouched with his legs spread, sipping a glass of red wine he'd poured from a small carafe. He had a gaudy ring on his slender middle finger. The big ruby, probably fake, was set in gold threads that reached up like spider legs to hold the stone in place. He lacked even a hint of self-consciousness, glancing with mild interest around the café at the other customers. He wasn't beautiful, but striking. He had pronounced cheekbones and dark, languid eyes, fringed with long lashes. He also had a boy's downy moustache. He must have been all of 18.

When I approached his table he looked up. At first he saw a monk. Then, after a little banter, he saw my interest and started to flirt. The shyness I remembered had disappeared—probably thanks to the wine. I told him I was new in Toledo and asked if he'd show me to a made-up address where someone waited in a sickbed. Outside I patted his back, brushed against him a couple of times, and once we'd turned a dark corner, I grabbed his crotch and he let me. A deep kiss got him hot and he dropped to his knees in front of me. The sight of his bobbing head, the feel of his wet, snug mouth should have done the trick in about 30 seconds. But after a minute, then two, nothing happened. Nothing. I can't say Bernardo's face flashed through my mind. But something about Bernardo. Some kind of comparison. Some sense of disappointment in the shop clerk because of Bernardo. Who knows? I pulled the boy to his feet and tried to get rid of him. He kept clinging and whining until finally he gave up, said, "Fuck you," and tripped off down the street.

I strolled back to the plaza, then away from the lights to the river, rank with the smell of mud and discarded carp left to rot by the old men who still came down to fish. I stood on the Alcántara Bridge and listened to the water lap heavily against the banks. I felt the massive Alcázar above me, jutting from the granite hillside, only its outline visible in the darkness. I remembered my father telling me the story of brave General Moscardó, who battled the Republican forces besieging Franco's army holed up in the fortress. Moscardó had sacrificed his son, who had been snatched by the enemy, rather than surrender the Alcázar.

"Would you do that Papa?" I'd asked, bracing myself to hear that the demands of Spain must come first.

My father had stroked my hair. We were sitting on the

park bench not far from our apartment building and the sky was as blue as the agate marbles in my room. "Not for the Generalissimo himself," my father answered.

I stayed on the bridge almost an hour before trudging back to Santo Domingo. It was nearly half past 2 and I was damned tired, but still I couldn't go to my cell. I paced the dark corridors of the first floor and through the chapel and courtyard, then climbed the stairs. But instead of heading to my own wing, I turned toward Bernardo's. I'd already fucked him over once that day with the lies I'd told him about Castro and the sick letter that I'd pounded out myself on the typewriter in Simon's office. I thought, *I should leave him alone now. Leave him the hell alone.* But I knocked on his door all the same.

Eighteen
BERNARDO

Something moved on the bottom of the bed. *Rats from the cellar*, that was my first thought. Baroja had been making a fuss about them. Exterminators had come three times. First with poison, then cages. I had hoped the monastery was finally rid of the rodents. I shivered at the thought of one crossing my feet and kicked at it under the covers. Then came a meow. Followed by laughter.

"*Que pasa*, Bernardo? Having a nightmare?" Juan Ramón laughed again.

"Very funny." I raised myself up on my elbows. Juan Ramón stood at the infirmary door, his arms crossed, looking very satisfied with himself. When I held out my hand, the cat walked up my legs to inspect it.

"Recognize her?" Juan Ramón said. "It's the mother from outside the walls. The kittens are all over kingdom come by now."

The cat did seem to be the one we'd found near the crate the day we were jogging. She was black with a white spot above her eye. "She's scrawny now." The cat licked my hand with her sandpaper tongue. "Where did you find her?"

"Around the same place. I went jogging this morning. How are you feeling?"

"Better, I guess." I coughed and sat up so I could lean back against the wall.

"*Claro!* Sounds like it." Juan Ramón came in and sat on the bed next to mine. "At least it's warmer in here than it was last night."

The infirmary was long and narrow, occupying the space of five or six cells. It faced the east side of the monastery, and in the mornings the winter sun poured in through the tall windows. But once the sun climbed to its zenith, the usual chill returned. Santo Domingo had never been able to afford the baseboard heating units advised by a kind contractor who had offered to install them free of charge. And when the infirmary was empty, the heating units would have been wasted anyway. Now they would have brought more than a little comfort. Temperatures had been dipping to near freezing at night. Juan Ramón had brought me an extra blanket the night before.

"You shouldn't be here." I grabbed a tissue from the

nightstand and blew my nose. "Sebastián will be bringing my breakfast. What time is it?"

"Almost 8 o'clock."

The cat sauntered across the nightstand to Juan Ramón's lap. When he scratched behind her ears, she lifted her chin and he moved his fingers there. "I think I'll keep her."

"I'm sure Baroja will be thrilled about that." I sneezed and blew my nose again.

"*Pobrecito!*" Juan Ramón leaned over and stroked my arm as though it were another cat.

"Really. You shouldn't be here."

"You're sick, Bernardo. What kind of scandal can I cause? You think Baroja will think we're fucking our brains out between your coughing fits?" As he scratched the cat's back, she settled into his lap and purred.

I put my finger to my lips and glanced toward the door. "I don't know. I just want to be safe."

"You can't be safe and live."

"Maybe that's why I'm dying."

"Maybe." Juan Ramón raised his calm eyes from the cat to me.

"I just want it to be over."

"Ordination?"

"All of it. Baroja's surveillance, for one. You know, he stops in here three times a day. He might be on his way now."

"Visiting a sick monk is not surveillance, Bernardo." He went back to stroking the cat. "It's all in your power."

"Nothing is in my power."

"Everything is."

I sighed and looked up at the ceiling. "No wonder I'm sick."

"No wonder," Juan Ramón agreed.

The dumbwaiter screeched open just outside the door. The cat sprang from Juan Ramón's lap and leaped on top of a tall cabinet near the window. It was too late for Juan Ramón to leave the room without being noticed, so he went out into the hall to greet the old monk, and came back in with a tray of breakfast. Sebastián hobbled in after him. He was 80 and frail. His face seemed almost skeletal, except for a fleshy, bluish nose.

"*Buenos Días*, Brother," I said.

He nodded and slowly wheeled a cart to my bed. Juan Ramón deposited the tray upon it.

"Brother Arturo said to drink the broth, Bernardo." Sebastián lifted a lid from a small ceramic bowl. "It's good for you. It made me well."

Sebastián had stayed sick for almost two weeks in the cold, drafty infirmary, his fragile body pressed to the mattress by all the woolen blankets piled on him. I'd brought up his meals for several days before succumbing to the virus myself. Then he recovered and returned the favor.

"I'd better be going," Juan Ramón said. He quickly scooped up the cat while Sebastián was busy with my tray and winked at me. "It's all in your power," he called over his shoulder as he left the room.

Three months of Juan Ramón in my life suddenly seemed like years. Or days. I still can't say which. Baroja's pitying, watchful glances, real or imagined. Remorse. Longing that made me renounce my flesh, then indulge it sweetly with *him* deep inside of me. The relentless drumbeat, driving me to an impossible decision. All of these seemed to last for years. But the secret moments with Juan Ramón slipped away quickly. And so did the moments of ecstasy before my other lover, naked and crucified and lifting me to him above the high altar. When I finally got sick in February after three months of struggle, a sweet exhaustion carried me away from it all.

The next morning a strange vibrating sound woke me up. It was still dark, and when I followed the sound to a yellow-orange glow, I remembered that Baroja had finally brought in a space heater the night before. I imagined it was a fire blazing in a hearth and fell back to sleep. At about 8 o'clock, Sebastián hobbled in with my breakfast. I ate the boiled egg and the sugared *churros* the cook had made for me as a treat and drank the bowl of warm milk. I didn't feel weak or queasy anymore, but I didn't want to leave the infirmary.

I'd almost fallen back asleep when my father showed up. He'd never come to Santo Domingo. I immediately thought something had happened to my mother. He told me she was fine, but I found out later that once again his and my idea of truth weren't the same. He was dressed in a navy suit. The collar of his crisp white shirt cut into his doughy neck. His sweet cologne made me queasy. I asked him to open a window.

"What? In this cold?"

I threw off the blanket and started to get up.

"*Muy bien*, I'll do it. Stay there." He opened a window just a crack. It was a windy day and the cold air immediately rushed in. "You're sure it's not too much?"

"No. It's perfect."

He remained near the window, inspecting the room.

"Can I smoke in here?" he finally said, reaching into his breast pocket.

"No. It's an infirmary."

"What's the matter? Aren't you happy to see me? I came when I found out you were sick."

I said nothing.

"Things will change." He sat in a chair near a small cupboard that held towels and sponges. "You want them to, don't you?"

"Some things, yes." I was thinking of the last bruise my mother had tried to hide from me.

"I'm a believer in change, Bernardo. The first steps are always the hardest."

I squeezed my eyes shut and inhaled the cold air blowing in through the window. What did he want with me? Why didn't he just leave me alone?

"You know," he said, "I've been dreaming a little. That's always dangerous for me, because what I want usually comes true, and then there's more work. That goes for changes at the factories, updates, I mean, new technology. It goes for investments too. You make them and then you watch stock prices, keep an eye on your broker. People are out for themselves. You've got to watch them." He paused. "Guess what I've been dreaming about lately."

"I don't know, Father." I thought if I kept my eyes closed he might go away.

"I didn't think you would. That's no surprise, I'm beginning to realize. Things have to be put into words. All right, then. You're my son. That should tell you everything. A son means something to a father. An only son, especially. There are certain traditions between fathers and sons. To hell with the past, right? Long live tradition."

I opened my eyes and found my father gazing at me as casually as if conversations like this one were daily affairs.

"I want to tell you a story, Bernardo, about me and your grandfather. This happened when I was just 14—already a man of the world." He laughed. "Papa and I took the train to Barcelona to pick up a Mercedes that had been shipped there. His tailor shop was doing well. High profits for three years running. He wanted a car. Not a sports car. A sedan, a big sedan. I have a picture of it in my office. You've seen it, haven't you?"

"Yes." I felt strangely uncomfortable, almost frightened, though I wasn't sure why.

"He kept it for 20 years. Would never let anyone else drive it. Not that I wanted to, a monster of a car like that. Give me something sleek, with some zip. Something to impress the *chicas, que no?*" He winked. "*Entonces*, in Barcelona Papa and I checked in at a little hotel. I was starving, but he wanted to get the damned car before we ate. So we picked it up. Papa paid with cash. He'd kept the wad of bills in his trousers the whole way. Looked like an overgrown cock. He probably liked that. Anyway, that night we drove down by the docks, to this hotel off an alley. Drunks were pissing in the shadows and Papa decided to park the car out on the street. What did he care if people saw us go into the place? No one knew us."

"A brothel?" I said.

"*Claro!* My friend here was already jumping around at the sight of the place." He patted his crotch. "So we go in and a woman with boobs out to here greets us at the door. She's in this black, lacy thing that looks more like underwear than a dress. *Dios!* I would have gone with her then and there, old as she was. But she calls to a girl smoking near the bar. Tall, probably 10 years older than

I was. So this Camilla—that was her name—struts over to us. She smells just the way you think a whore would smell. You know what Papa asks?"

I shook my head.

" 'She clean?' " He laughed hard, showing all his yellow teeth under his moustache. "She clean?" he repeated to himself. "*Sabes*—Papa was a very practical man."

"Was she?"

He shrugged. "Hell, I didn't care. I didn't know what I do now. But I didn't pick up anything from her. So, I go upstairs with her, to this room with the lights low—red mantillas over the lamp shades. She strips for me, real slow. By the time she's through my pants are wet. But she was a sweet piece, I'll tell you that. An ass like some kind of soft pastry. I could have eaten it too. We went at it three times. Hell, I was young. I'll bet she made Papa pay extra." He grinned.

My head ached. I drank some water from the glass on the nightstand.

"Afterward in the car Papa says, '*Dimme, Hijo*, how was your first lay?' You know what I tell him? I say, 'The lay was good, Papa, but it sure as hell wasn't my first.' How do you like that, Bernardo? *Que sorpresa!* You should have seen his eyes—like saucers. Then he cusses at me for wasting his money and we laugh. We laugh all the way home."

"That's tradition?" I said.

He leaned forward, his elbows on his knees. "You and I missed that kind of thing. Maybe we got off on the wrong foot." He squinted slyly at me. "I'm willing to bet that you've never been laid. Stuck in a place like this your whole life. *Tengo razón, que no?* 26... 27, and never been laid.

Now, that's a real sin. Better visit the confessional, Bernardo."

"I'm a monk," I said weakly. "I'm going to be ordained in a few months."

Father straightened. His expression became serious. "There's no honor lost in leaving a place like this. They operate under different rules. They don't even believe in honor. Why do you think you're sick?" He stood up, walked to the window, and looked out. Then he shut the door and sat back down in the chair. He leaned forward on his knees, eyeing me intensely. "I want to ask you something. Has anyone been bothering you?"

"Bothering me?"

"Strange phone calls, notes, things like that."

I shook my head, completely puzzled.

"Anyone strange hanging around?"

"In the monastery?"

"I mean on the streets, when you're out."

"No. Why? What are you worried about?" He actually did seem nervous, glancing toward the door, tugging on his tie.

"Ah, it's nothing." He waved his hand and got up. "Goddamned rumors, that's all. Forget about it. And remember what I said: Get the hell out of here, *Hijo*, before they get both your balls."

When he left, I had the urge to run after him. Not really because I wanted to clear up the mystery. I knew he wouldn't tell me anything else. Maybe I had some vague sense that there would be no more conversations—though I couldn't have had even the slightest awareness of how everything would end. It was just that in that moment I wished things had turned out differently between us.

Other possibilities glimmered through some of my memories, like sunlight flashing now and then into a car passing under the leafy branches up in the Pyrenees. Once, in Cádiz when I was 5 or 6, the ocean current had pulled me under the water and carried me what seemed to be the length of a soccer field from the shore. I couldn't touch bottom. My father had taught me to dog paddle but I panicked and began bobbing, salt water rushing into my mouth, burning my eyes. I mouthed the word "Mama" over and over, though no real sound came out, and before long slipped under the waves. Then someone yanked me by the arm. My head broke through the surface and my father pulled me into his arms and carried me toward the shore. "You're all right, *Hijo*," he gently repeated until we'd cleared the waves. He tried to set me down on a towel my frantic mother had spread, but I kept clutching his neck.

Maybe the man who'd just visited me was the same one who'd rescued me that day at the ocean. Maybe he understood the natural order. And maybe for all his faults, he would be forgiven because he had remained faithful to it. Remained faithful? No, that suggested volition. My father lived by instinct. The *right* instinct, not the one driving me. The Church said so. Society said so. Father's brothel story would make the old monks roar. Maybe it would make the Pope himself roar. A man will be a man.

• • •

Later that week, when I'd left the infirmary, my mother called and repeated my father's strange question.

"Are you all right?" she said. "There's no one bothering you?"

"That's what Father asked me. What's going on?"

"I don't know," she said. "I wish I did. Maybe it's a dream. When did you speak to your father?"

I told her about the conversation in the infirmary.

She sighed. "You're not keeping anything from me? You don't have to protect me."

"Really, I'm fine." What was the source of all this, I wondered? In that moment, I thought of Juan Ramón's letter. Could there be some kind of connection? Was his sick stalker trying to get to him through me? But it didn't make any sense. Why go through my parents? I dismissed the idea.

"I want to see you, Bernardo. Come for the *comida* on Sunday."

"*Muy bien*, Mama. I'll be there."

"Be careful."

When I arrived at the house on Sunday I went right up to my old room to change before going to find my mother. She kept a wardrobe for me so I could get out of my habit every now and then. I slipped off the robe and hung it in the closet. Starched shirts and pressed trousers hung neatly. Loafers, oxfords, and tennis shoes rested in orderly rows on the shelves above. I put on a white monogrammed shirt, pleated trousers, and a pair of soft oxfords. The shoes felt tight, but I knew it was because my feet were used to sandals.

My old room hadn't been rearranged since I'd gone away to minor seminary at the age of 14. Glass-doored bookcases were lined with my favorite childhood stories, reference books, and volumes my mother had purchased for me after I entered seminary. There was no place for them in my tiny cell at Santo Domingo, and I liked to thumb through them when I came home for a visit. Like my mother, I especially liked biographies of saints and spiritual journals, and they filled several shelves. The spacious room held a large desk, armchairs, and a double bed. The plaster walls were bright, decorated with a heavy carved crucifix and several paintings of the sea that Mother had bought on vacations to Cádiz when I was a little. The room's large windows looked out onto the gardens. Even in February they were lush with shrubs and holly trees, and some early jonquils made bright yellow patches among the green foliage. The cold weather of the previous week had given way to warm currents blowing up from Africa, so the windows were opened wide and a breeze rustled the drapes.

I stepped into my bathroom to comb my hair. I was supposed to join my mother at 2 o'clock. I had always looked forward to this monthly Sunday meal with her. Sometimes my *abuela* Esteban came and sometimes my maternal grandfather and his crusty nurse. Sometimes when my grandmother was there, my father deigned to join us. Today, however, it was just my mother and me.

When I arrived in Madrid that day I'd stopped at a street vendor and bought Mama a bouquet of white greenhouse roses. Anna had taken them from me at the door and when I went downstairs I found them in a crystal vase on the foyer table. I carried them to the terrace, where I found my mother seated under a large umbrella. Her lavender skirt rippled in the wind and a lavender sweater was thrown over her shoulders. Her dark hair was swept back and tightly coiled. When she turned to me, I saw the purplish bruise around her left eye. The lid was swollen.

"When did this happen?" I set the vase on the wrought-iron table and bent over to inspect her eye.

She shook her head and moved my hand from her chin and kissed it. "I'm fine. It's nothing."

"*Dios*, Mama. You have to get away from him."

She brushed away my words with a wave of her hand and looked at the roses. "How lovely," she said. "Thank you, *Hijo*."

I sighed in exasperation and sat. It was no use pushing her. She began rearranging the flowers in the vase.

"Anna has no eye for this," she said.

I sat back, hating him and angry with her for playing the martyr. Finally she pushed the vase away and settled back too.

"Your father has me scared to death, Bernardo."

I started to go off, but she put her hand on my mouth.

"It's not this," she said, quietly. "It's his strange preoccupation about being followed or harassed or whatever it is. And if he has gotten you mixed up in anything..."

"So, *he's* the one in trouble?" I felt disappointed despite myself. Why should I have ever believed he'd come to my sickbed to offer solace?

She sighed. "I've been thinking about it for the past two days. It must have something to do with business. But your father has never involved you in business matters. Something is not quite right. He wanted to know if you'd seen anybody strange loitering around the monastery or the school. I told him you'd mentioned nothing to me. So he went to you himself."

"I told him nobody was bothering me."

"He's in some kind of trouble. I've never seen him so

restless. He paces out here on the terrace like a nervous watchdog. He loses his temper."

"He's never needed an excuse for that."

"It's worse. He's been drinking. That's how this happened." She motioned to her face. "He was so sorry afterward. He cried like a baby."

"Please, Mother."

"He gave me a gun."

"What?!"

She reached into her purse and pulled out a pistol so small it fit in the palm of her hand. I took it from her. The only gun I'd ever touched was the revolver that Father kept in his office. He'd shown me how to shoot it when I was 9 or 10. This one wasn't even half as big. It was delicate and no heavier than an orange. I checked to make sure there was a safety catch. There was. The chamber held four cartridges.

"He told me to keep it in my purse. But it makes me nervous. Would you put it somewhere?"

"He thinks you should have a gun. If you're in danger…"

She shook her head. "Who would want to hurt me? Or you?"

I was at a complete loss. "If he thinks you should have a gun, maybe you ought to."

"No. Please, put it somewhere."

Giving in, I carried the pistol into the salon and laid it in an olive wood box my mother kept on a console behind a sofa.

When Anna stepped out to the terrace and announced that dinner was ready, we made our way to the dining room. Our places had been set at one end of the large table. Pedro poured the wine and brought us onion soup.

I said a blessing. We talked about my ordination.

"Do you know what makes me sad?" Mother said, suddenly wistful. "To think that you and I may never take another trip together. To the sea, I mean, to Cádiz like in the old days. Or even abroad to France or Italy.

I smiled. "We can still take trips, Mama. Even if I'm assigned to Salamanca, I can go on vacations."

She brightened. "You know, I found you the perfect ordination gift."

"What is it?"

She shook her finger at me. "It's a secret, dear. But I think it's something you'll treasure."

Later I learned that she'd bought me a silver pyx for taking communion to the sick. It was embossed with the Greek *chi-rho*, the Christogram.

"Of course I will." *If there is an ordination*, I silently added. What would she do if Baroja denied my application? What would she think if she knew the reason?

She said nothing more that afternoon about the conversation with Father, but she asked me to let Enrique, the driver, take me back to the monastery. And when she gave me a parting embrace she said, "Be careful, son."

It was already dark when the car pulled up to Santo Domingo, and the bells were ringing for vespers. In the chapel most of the monks had already taken their places in the choir. They were reading the office for the day or saying their rosaries. Juan Ramón wasn't there yet. I wondered how he had spent the afternoon. I wished more than anything we could walk together in the sunlight instead of creeping around at night like vampires.

I knelt at my place and tried to collect myself. Brother

Ricardo was playing the *Pangue Lingua* on the organ's flutiest pipes. *Sing my tongue, the Savior's glory.* The words floated through my mind like dust motes dancing in a shaft of sunlight. On the altar, candles glowed around the gold monstrance ready to receive the sacred host for adoration—Christ himself, food of Angels. Just as the music stopped, Juan Ramón entered the choir, genuflected, and took his seat. He opened his breviary. Why was he not looking for me? Suddenly my chest felt constricted and I could hardly breathe. Baroja announced the opening invitation, "Oh God, come to my assistance." I watched the 10 monks in the opposite stalls make the sign of the cross. I waited. Juan Ramón gazed at me now, and I could breathe again.

Nineteen

JUAN RAMÓN

How fucking long would he be in there? It felt like hours had passed on the dark street outside Esteban's house. I waited in Simon's car. For all practical purposes it belonged to me since the crippled old man could hardly walk, let alone drive. It was the night I'd specified in the last letter, the signed letter—as though Esteban needed a signature by now. I'd sent it after I'd given up trying to find Entralgo. I figured Esteban could lead me to him, with enough incentive. Restless, I drummed the steering wheel with my fingers and checked my watch for the hundredth time. It was almost a quarter to midnight, the stipulated hour. Maybe it had all fallen through. Maybe Esteban had his own plans.

But when headlights appeared on the long drive, my hopes revived. The car slowly advanced, stopping a moment at the gate, which slid open. When the sedan rounded a curve a hundred meters away, I followed it to the Paseo del Prado and then down the avenue that led to Puerto del Sol. The plaza buzzed with life. Lights glowed in cafés and shops, which were packed. Pedestrians passed to and from the subway exit and gathered in groups on the sidewalks. Steady streams of people along the side streets made their way to Plaza Mayor, only a few blocks away. Passing through the crowded area, Esteban's sedan turned down a narrow street that wove through government buildings with Renaissance facades. It headed into an old neighborhood crowded with apartment buildings. Finally the car stopped at one of them, and the driver opened the back door for Esteban. He climbed out and glanced around. He wore a suit and carried a briefcase. He surveyed the building in front of him. Most of the windows were dark. After giving some instructions to the driver, he started for the building.

When he had climbed the stone stairs and opened the front door, I got out of the car and crossed the street. I strolled up to the door as though I'd been out for an evening walk. In the darkness, there was little chance the driver would recognize me from my visit to the Esteban house, especially since I was not in my habit. I didn't want to appear uncertain in front of the driver, so I pretended to collect my mail from one of the boxes in the hallway while I watched Esteban enter an apartment down the dark hall. Then I followed, standing outside the door.

"What in the hell is this?" Esteban yelled. "You threaten me and then don't want my money? Are you a lunatic?"

"I must be if I sent that kind of letter. Look at me, for God's sake. I haven't been out of this wheelchair in 10 years." Invalid or not, Entralgo's voice was firm and loud.

"I should kill you anyway," Esteban said. "Maybe you are crazy. Maybe you want to cause trouble for me?"

"Go to the devil. I've got other things to think about besides you."

"You know what I think?" Esteban lowered his voice. "I think you don't have a thing to think about except dying. You've got some thug going after your old acquaintances for fun. First Castro, now Esteban. The bastard cheated me out of the cut I deserved for the job, that's what you're thinking."

"Castro? What would I have to do with his death? You think I have the money to pay someone?" Entralgo's voice quavered now. "Castro was always opening his mouth. He pissed off so many people they were probably standing in line to cut him."

The apartment was silent for a moment. Maybe Esteban was studying the invalid, deciding whether to believe him.

I moved back from the door and climbed halfway up the dark back stairs where I'd be hidden if Esteban suddenly emerged.

Within seconds, the door flew open. I leaned back against the wall. Footsteps pounded down the hallway and the front door of the building opened and clicked shut. I waited for a couple of minutes, then descended the stairs and approached Entralgo's door, still ajar. Through the space between the jamb and the door, I caught a glimmer of the wheelchair and Entralgo's motionless form. Entralgo's head was on his chest, his large body slumped forward. Blood spilled from his throat onto his dingy white shirt.

• • •

"You heard it yourself on the news," I said to Bernardo. "Entralgo's dead." Once again it was dark and once again we were at Cristo de la Luz.

"You're sure he's the same man? You're sure?"

"I know the name, goddamn it. And I sure as hell know the face."

"But after 20 years?"

"You think I could forget it?" I squeezed his arm hard. I didn't have to pretend to be angry. "It's burned into my mind. It'll be there until I take my last breath."

We sat on the stone steps at the head of the mosque. For a moment we said nothing. It had begun to rain and when cars passed us, the stillness was broken by the sound of water spraying beneath their wheels. March had come. I could smell the wet wool of Bernardo's habit. I could see traces of streetlight on his face, still full of innocence but now alive with lust for me. Yes, lust, goddamn it. I won't beatify him into a Spanish mystic, part of a long line of repressed Carmelites. Lust means you get hot the way God intended. You want to fuck and be fucked. But it's not a choice of hard sweltering flesh over hard icy soul, pristine as a frozen peak in a rarified atmosphere. The soul fires the eyes, works the muscles toward another human being. The soul is the embrace, hard flesh inside of warm wet flesh.

The soul is the longing and the consummation. Don't tell me differently.

And then there was the bastard Esteban. Ready to piss himself from fear. Always looking over his shoulder. Cutting a fucking invalid.

And now he knew it wasn't Castro or Entralgo. No, some unknown sniper eyeing him from the rooftops of Madrid high-rises, waiting around the corner at restaurants. Watching him. Watching his son: Some of the notes told him so. Why not? I wanted to see if he could muster a father's feelings. If so, that was one more fear. But his arrogance was too big to let him care for much beyond his own skin.

Did it ever occur to him that it was the Fuertes boy? Did he regret letting me live? Possibly. Maybe he was even trying to hunt me down. Maybe he'd eventually find me. Exciting idea. But it would be too fucking late before he did.

"Do you know what I hate about this, Bernardo?" I finally said. "Even more than knowing someone is out there ready to kill me?" I was steeling myself against him. I had to. But everything I told him that night was the truth. At least all the important things. "It gives me nightmares. About my own parents. I don't mean the kind of nightmares I had after it happened. I mean nightmares about who they were. They look different in them. They look at me in a way they never looked at me. Like I am a stranger to them. Like they feel sorry for me. Not deeply. I'm only distracting them temporarily from something. My parents, Bernardo."

I got up and went to the window, watched the rain falling on a tile roof that reflected the streetlight. "You know, I remember once my mother was reaching for something in the kitchen, up on the cupboard. She was standing on a stool and she fell. When I ran over to help her, she looked at me as if she were annoyed. Her look in the dreams is something like that."

Bernardo came over to me and put his arm around me. My muscles tensed. I pulled away. My head had started to pound. I couldn't do this now. "I'm going back to the monastery," I said. "I want to go back by myself."

Bernardo stepped away from me and let me pass. I walked slowly down the hillside to the small Plaza de San Nicolás. I stepped under an awning to get out of the rain. My hair and habit were soaked. My sandals felt like sponges beneath my feet. I took out my handkerchief and wiped the rain off my face. I heard someone running across the cobblestones and looked up to see Bernardo coming toward me. When he reached the awning, he stopped, panting.

"Let me go back with you," he said.

I nodded. "Race me back."

I sprinted across the Plaza and down the narrow Calle Cadenas. By the time I reached the well-lit Calle Comercio I could hear Bernardo behind me. I sped forward, my habit heavy with rain, leaping over a puddle in the street. Bernardo's footsteps continued to echo behind me. When I cut across the Plaza del Ayuntamiento before the cathedral a man carrying an umbrella jumped out of my path. I felt a second wind come. Adrenaline surged through me. I breathed easily, my sandals furiously slapping the wet stones. Lorca's words ran through my head, beating out the pace of my strides. *The cry of the guitar begins...It weeps for things distant...the arrow without target...the evening without morning...and the first bird death upon the branch, weep...The cry of the guitar...* My feet kicked up behind me as I rounded the corner down from Santo Domingo. I raced toward the silhouette of the chapel's towers. I bounded up the steps of the monastery's entrance and stopped, my chest heaving. I doubled over to catch my breath. A few moments later, Bernardo ran up the stairs and stopped next to me.

"We're not through yet," Bernardo said, panting. He opened the front door with his key. "Come on, all the way to your cell." He turned and released the door.

I grabbed it before it could shut. I raced through the dark entrance hall behind Bernardo and then passed him as we came to the staircase, taking the stairs two at a time. I made it to my cell just ahead of him, collapsing on the bed. Bernardo closed the door and dropped down beside me in the dark room.

"I win?" I said, struggling to catch my breath.

Bernardo nodded, throwing his head back on the pillow. I climbed on top of him, straddling him on my knees.

"I win?" I said again, shaking him by the arms.

"Yes. I said, yes." Bernardo coughed.

I got up and pulled Bernardo to his feet. I untied the cord around his habit and slipped the wet robe over his head. I pushed him back onto the bed and took off my habit. I climbed onto him. His skin was damp with the rain and sweat. It was soft. He lay passively beneath my hands. I began to move with determination, even force. I moved as though I had to subdue an animal, directing Bernardo's legs, arms this way and that, sliding him, shoving him. My body beat against his. *The cry of the guitar...* someone, a woman, seemed to scream the words inside my head...*the cry of the guitar...grievously wounded by five knives!*

We lay there afterward, listening to the rain, my chest against his back. The moment had arrived.

"There's something I want to show you," I said. "I mean I have to show you or else...never mind, I just have to show you." I went to the desk. My heart pounded. I turned on the lamp, opened the drawer, and took out another typed letter. "Here."

Bernardo sat up and read it, shaking his head. "This has got to stop. You've got to go to the police."

"It's Entralgo."

"What?"

"At first I thought maybe Castro was sending the letters. But then Castro was killed and the letters kept coming. This came two days ago. Before Entralgo died."

Bernardo shrugged. "So if he's the one, he won't be harassing you anymore."

"Because he was killed. And he says Castro's killer will come after me. The name is right there." I pointed to the letter. "Castro's killer—he says it."

Bernardo looked at the letter. The confusion on his face gave way to understanding. "*Dios!*" he said. "But maybe it's just another sick threat."

"He was killed, Bernardo. There *is* someone out there."

"Then you have to tell the police. My God, Juan Ramón, what are you waiting for?"

I shook my head. "It wouldn't do any good. I know who it is. I've suspected it for a while, but now I know. It's the third man. The one who held me while the other two killed my mother and father. He ordered them to do it. I can still smell the cologne on his hand. He was covering my mouth." I hesitated. "It's your father, Bernardo. I recognized him the minute I saw him again. The minute I smelled his cologne. I'm not mistaken. I know him. And now he knows me."

Bernardo just stared at me.

"He killed Castro and Entralgo. Now he's coming for me. That's what it says." I motioned to the letter and quoted from it again, " 'Castro's killer will come for you. You'll burn in hell with Mama and Papa.' The letter came the day before Entralgo died. He must have sent letters like that to your father. That's the best I can figure. You saw what it did to him. That's what made him so jumpy. First your father suspected Castro and killed him. When the letters kept coming he knew it was Entralgo. He had to keep Entralgo's mouth shut. He plans to do the same to me."

Bernardo looked at me as if I was playing a cruel joke on him. "Why are you saying this? Why my father?"

I felt myself faltering, but I took a deep breath and continued. "I'm telling you. I recognized him the minute I set eyes on him. And now he's figured out who I am. With Entralgo's help, I guess. I don't know how the hell Entralgo found me or when. Maybe he's always kept track of me. It doesn't change what I feel for you, I swear. I know you had nothing to do with it. You hate him too, for Christ's sake."

Bernardo pressed his hands to his ears when I started to go on. He got up and fumbled into his habit. I stood and grabbed him by the arms. "You know what I have to do. Before it's too late. The police wouldn't believe me. I have to act. That's why I'm telling you. You have to understand."

"Why are you doing this?" He spoke in a strained whisper. His defective eyes were full of pain, as though I were playing a cruel game.

"I'm not lying." I shook him. "You don't believe me? Castro and Entralgo are dead. Your father did it. He knows about me. What choice do I have? Do I sit here and wait for him?"

His eyes widened and he pulled away from me. "You can't commit murder."

"Think of what he did. Think of it. I have, every fucking day of my life."

"You *want* to do this. You really want to make somebody pay. My God, Juan Ramón."

"What if I do?" I shouted. "What do you expect? And I'll risk life in prison if I have to."

"No." Bernardo shook his head. "I don't believe it. I want out of here." He left the cell. I heard him running down the corridor.

It was after 2 o'clock in the morning when I left Santo Domingo and crossed the plaza in front of the chapel's facade. Satchel in hand, I walked along Calle Alfonso X, past dark shops and the shadowy church of San Juan Bautista. A few couples still strolled through the plazas. Traffic on the streets was light. With the satchel on my lap, I rested on a bench in the small plaza just beyond the university. For a few minutes I gazed at the massive 16th-century edifice of stone and brick. Then I continued on to Santiago del Arrabal. I let myself into the church through the sacristy, reached through a dark passage well off the street. I hesitated at the light switch. *Better to stumble into the sanctuary than draw attention with bright windows*, I decided. I felt my way along the cupboards to the sanctuary door and stepped out before the altar. The sanctuary candle, suspended from a chain, cast its glow on the golden doors of the tabernacle. Once my eyes adjusted to the meager light, I deposited the satchel on the altar and walked down the long nave to the rear of the church. I lifted the copper lid from the baptismal font, a 14th century treasure, and carried it back to the sanctuary. The bowl-shaped lid rocked when I set it upside down on the altar, but it seemed steady enough. I opened the satchel and removed the folders containing the news-clippings about Esteban and my notes on Esteban and his two thugs. I dropped everything into the makeshift pot, except for one sheet of paper. That I rolled up and, stretching on tiptoe, lit it with the flame of the sanctuary candle. I brought the glowing punk to the altar and ignited the other papers. The blaze illuminated the details of the lowest panels on the reredos, the carved bodies of the apostles. The processional crucifix glowed on its stand and the now bright halo of stars encircling the Virgin left a shadow like a bite on the wall. I knelt before the altar and watched the flames gradually shrink and disappear. I prayed an *ave* for my mother and then one for my father. When everything was dark again and perfectly quiet, I put the church in order and went back to Santo Domingo.

Twenty

BERNARDO

Dios te salve Maria. Llena eres de gracia. El Señor es contigo... Ruega por nosotros pecadores... pecadores... pecadores. Sinners sinners sinners... Pray for us sinners.

Standing in the little curtained antechamber of the shower stall, I turned on the faucet and took off my bathrobe. I coughed hard and the sound reverberated against the tiled floor and walls of the large communal lavatory. The other four shower stalls were empty. Was anyone in the toilet stalls? What did I care? I inserted my hand under the spray. Chilly, I thought—not caring how cold it felt on my skin—thinking like a scientist examining a test tube, as though I must record the data. And then thinking of routine things. About how the boiler came on only after matins and during the evening recreation hour so the monks could shower after exercise, though few did besides me—the abbot and perhaps Brother Jaime, the librarian.

I usually showered in the evening, but I'd spent the past hour and a half racing my bicycle around Toledo's perimeter on a warm afternoon, peddling in a daze, and my skin was salty from perspiration. Did I even brace myself for the cold when I stepped into the stall? I only remember the water refreshed me. I closed my eyes and let the stream pound against my head, my chest, my back, and prayed. *Ruega por nosotros pecadores.* It was Holy Week. In the midst of everything, everything, I could lose myself in the rhythm of the somber chants, the drama of Christ's passion.

The night before was Holy Thursday, Baroja had washed the feet of 12 of the monks during mass, including mine and Juan Ramón's, who I'd sat next to.

When we bent down to remove a sandal our eyes met. Juan Ramón seemed to plead with me. But plead for what? For understanding? Support? Surely not for a promise. *Please come with me afterward:* Is that what he wanted me to hear? What hope was there for any kind of future?

It wasn't that doubts about Juan Ramón bubbled to the surface of my thoughts. Not then. Not yet. It would have been harder to believe that Juan Ramón had killed than that my father had. I *could* believe it about my father. I *could* believe his power to wound, to rationalize the most selfish whim he had. I *could* believe him capable of taking someone's life. Nor were there doubts about the web of information that Juan Ramón showed me—letters, threats, secrets, demented men. How could I begin to cope with that even if I were inclined to think of logistics? If any doubts lay beneath the surface, they were doubts about Juan Ramón's love for me: If he knew all along whose son I was, if he had known that, what could he have been thinking, hoping? Why wouldn't he hate me? When he slapped my bare buttocks, when he impaled me and rode me until I bled, when he gagged me with himself, what kind of desire was driving him? I couldn't begin to fathom all of Juan Ramón's reasons, the intricate calculations clicking away in his mind since he'd come to Santo Domingo. But ignorance was better. If only mine could be complete. Why had he revealed his plans to me? I tried to stop answering that question, and I wouldn't let myself stop believing that he loved me.

Maybe he wanted me to see a plea for forgiveness in that glance, for planning to murder my father. A plea that could be granted by a truly perfected monk. But I hated my father. What had I to forgive? It was no sin against me, nor against my mother, who would be saved. And I was too exhausted now, too resolved, to feel remorse for my hatred. My blood had thickened as though infected with some kind of disease that finally causes a catatonic state. The disease had stilled the frenetic waves of panic, of every desperate and scrupulous impulse that requires coursing blood. If Juan Ramón's glance had conveyed something more basic—*Don't protect him; Don't stop me*—even that request was unnecessary. My ability to act, except automatically, had escaped me.

I knew this after the Holy Thursday rituals. Baroja had stripped the linens from the altar and removed the blessed sacrament from the tabernacle. He had carried off the gold ciborium, the way the Roman guards at Gethsemane had carried off Christ, while we intoned the *Pangue Lingua*. *Sing my tongue the savior's glory...on the night of his last supper...* Thoughts of betrayal, of murder, lingered in my mind while I kept the first watch in the side chapel. I imagined Juan Ramón in a fetid Madrid prison. I imagined two burly prisoners holding down this priest who had committed murder while a third prisoner raped him. I was kneeling alone before the displaced ciborium when I heard footsteps behind me and then felt a hand on my shoulder. As predictably as the *Pangue Lingua* the motions unfolded, not a thought to sacrilege. I was numb even to the cold slates under us. I accepted Juan Ramón's tongue in my mouth with the same unflinching acceptance I gave to the sacred host during communion. I accepted Juan Ramón inside me, not with joy or excitement but with a sense of inevitability. When I felt his tears on my chest, I couldn't rally myself to comfort, even though I possessed comforting information, revealed to me only in that moment.

After the Good Friday service that afternoon, I left for Madrid. It was drizzling when I arrived. I hardly noticed as I walked from Atocha Station to my father's house. From time to time, I absently swiped at my wet face with my sleeve. I could not speak to Guillermo at the gate or to Pedro when he opened the front door.

Twenty-One
Juan Ramón

Goddamn it! Conscience or love or whatever was making me backtrack. That was my feeling at the time. Had I pushed him too far? Would he ever find his way out of the pit? After absolution, after the law let him go, if it ever did? But had I actually pushed him to it? Somewhere inside me I'd always figured I'd be the one to do it finally, as much as I tried to fuck up his mind, as much satisfaction as I told myself I'd get from that.

His mother's bruises were still fresh. Bernardo had told me about the beating. And about the gun. How simple to use it and claim defense or outrage. She'd back me. And even if she didn't, what jury who knew the whole story would put me away for life? Even if they did, I'd have won. I'd have finished it. So when I told Bernardo I planned to kill his father, it wasn't exactly a lie.

Then why had I confessed to him and risked exposure? A genuine risk, wasn't it? Of course I *knew* Bernardo's feelings for me. He'd let me go through with it, no matter what price he'd have to pay in guilt. Besides, knowing now what his father was capable of, would he risk my life by warning him? Would he go to Baroja or anyone to encourage surveillance of me, to deter me? Would he do this when he knew how fucking ridiculous it would sound? Even surveillance wouldn't have stopped me. Maybe he knew that. I would have killed Esteban anyway.

So why the attempt to use him, however lame? Why use Bernardo after everything between us? Why use him when I wanted him so badly? Those questions haunted me. To hurt him, Esteban's son? Wasn't that the goal all along? And of course imagining Esteban's face in the split second before his own son killed him. Or down deep was it empathy I wanted, from someone who already knew what Esteban was made of and hated him for it? That is, if Bernardo really hated his father. I doubted it. Resentment, anger, shame—these things Bernardo had felt. But he also longed for his father, just as any son longs for his father. Maybe it was that longing I wanted to destroy.

When I followed him to Madrid on Good Friday, I told myself it was to finish what he wouldn't be able to. I ran to the train station after I went to his cell and found him gone. I knew where he was going. He'd promised to go running with me at 10 o'clock, Baroja be damned. He'd come get me. When 10:30 came with no sign of him, I knew. I made a quick inspection of the chapel in case he was there and then checked with Diego, who'd seen him leave. I got out of my running clothes, changed into jeans. I'd seen him at 9:30. Starting at 10:30 the trains left at 30 minute intervals. He'd probably taken the 10:30 train to Madrid. Or maybe he'd missed it and was waiting for the 11 o'clock.

I got to the station just as the 11 o'clock pulled up to the platform. I saw him board. I climbed into the car behind him.

A light rain started up just as the train pulled into Madrid. From Atocha to the Esteban house, I stayed 20 meters behind him. He wore jeans and a red sweatshirt. Twice he looked back, but he didn't seem to see me.

The impulse to run up and stop him never left me. But I wouldn't do it. I just wouldn't. Some stubborn voice inside kept me from it. The real reason, I know now, was that to stop him would amount to a declaration—for me it would have. It would be a pledge to him that I could never retract. And I was fucking frozen at the thought of it.

But when I saw him through the iron palings, advancing to the front door, my movements became liquid and fast as a stream. Because I was ready to do it—to pledge myself. I knew I was. Then I couldn't stand being on the other side of the fence. I beat on the guardhouse door to get Guillermo's attention. He was on the phone. He held up his finger for me to wait. He talked another full minute until I started pounding again and he finally sauntered over. I had to tell him who I was. He scratched his head until he remembered me and finally opened the gate. "I have to announce you, Father!" he called after me. But I was already sprinting up the drive. When no one came to the door for all my pounding, I knew. I knew it was too late. When the butler finally opened the door, he stammered at me. His face was blanched. He pointed toward Esteban's office. When I got there I found Bernardo and his mother kneeling over Esteban, who was face down on the floor. The telephone receiver dangled from the desk, just over his head. Blood oozed from his white shirt, pooling on the marble floor. Because of his red sweatshirt, Bernardo seemed to be covered in the blood. I ran to him and pried the gun out of his hand. His mother was white, trembling. When I took the gun, she started to sob.

• • •

Inspector Duran was a serious looking man in his mid 40s. He was also short, which made the dandruff on the shoulders of his black suit all the more conspicuous to someone as tall as me. Baroja had greeted Duran and his assistant Lieutenant Cervantes at the door of his office. Cervantes was a heavy-set man with bags under his brown eyes. He reminded me of a drowsy basset hound. Baroja introduced Bernardo and me to the pair. They sat in the two armchairs across from the desk. Bernardo and I had pulled up straight-back chairs Baroja kept against the wall. Baroja sat behind his desk.

"*Entonces*, Father." Duran motioned to Cervantes who took a pad and pen from the breast pocket of his jacket. "You were out of the monastery last Friday morning?"

"Yes, Inspector. I was helping the pastor out at Santa Teresa. We were preparing for Stations of the Cross."

"And that afternoon Brother Bernardo came to you immediately?"

Baroja looked at Bernardo, who stared solemnly ahead. He hadn't looked at me once. "Yes. I left the church immediately when I got word. Brother Bernardo told me he'd explained everything to the police when they arrived at his parents' house. Afterward."

"*Sí. Verdad.* This is part of our formal inquest. It's required in every homicide case."

"I understand." Baroja clearly wished the matter could end. I'd found out from Diego, not Bernardo, that Bernardo had broken down in the abbot's office on Friday afternoon. Baroja had been understanding, had embraced Bernardo and let him sob. They'd talked for over an hour and when Bernardo came out he looked relieved. It wasn't until later that Bernardo told me Baroja had promised him he'd be ordained. Sheer pity probably explained it. We'd been discrete enough, but only an idiot or a blind man would have failed to see we'd continued meeting. Of course Bernardo had probably made some little declaration about celibacy, about us. And evidently Baroja had believed him.

"Just one more thing, Father," Duran said, his little black rodent eyes glimmering. "Have you met Señora Esteban?"

"Yes, Inspector. She is a very good woman. She's been very generous to the monastery."

"Have you noticed bruises on her face in the past?"

Baroja lowered his eyes a moment, embarrassed. He cleared his throat and raised his head. "I'm afraid so, Inspector. I wish we'd have done something."

Duran smiled sympathetically. "You know what they say about hindsight, Father." He stopped Cervantes from writing down his remark. "Now, Brother Bernardo." He turned to Bernardo, who was sitting next to Cervantes. "I realize Officer Alvarez already questioned you and Father Fuertes in my absence. However, I would like to take your statement myself. Please forgive the repetition."

Bernardo nodded. He seemed tranquil enough. His color was good. His strabismic eyes were bright. Why not? He'd gone running back to Baroja's skirts like a good penitent.

"You arrived at your parents' home just before noon, then? Eleven-fifty, according to the man at the front gate."

"Yes. I took the 11 o'clock train."

"You didn't call your mother first. Is that unusual?"

"No. Sometimes I like to surprise her."

"You knew she would be home that morning?"

"No, not for certain. But Good Friday services don't start until mid afternoon. It seemed likely that she'd still be home."

"I see." Duran glanced over at Cervantes to make sure he was recording the responses.

"Tell me exactly what happened."

Bernardo took a deep breath. "When I went into the salon, Mother wasn't there."

Duran interrupted by raising his hand. "How did you get into the house? Do you have a key?"

Bernardo shook his head. "Pedro let me in."

"The butler."

"Yes."

"And where did Pedro go after he let you in?"

"I don't know. Probably back to his rooms behind the kitchen."

The burly Alvarez had questioned Guillermo and old Pedro individually and in private, just as he'd questioned

Bernardo, Señora Esteban, and me. The maid had been away running errands. So Bernardo really didn't know where Pedro had gone—at the time. What he didn't tell Duran is that before the police came, before he, his mother, and I decided on the "facts," we'd consulted with the butler. After letting in Bernardo he'd returned to his apartment and was there when he heard the shot. He'd seen or heard nothing leading up to it.

"Go on."

"When I didn't find Mother in the salon, I started to go up to her room. That's when I heard Father yelling. I ran down the corridor to father's office."

Duran stopped Bernardo again. "Why didn't you go to your father's office right away on coming home?"

"I thought he was out of town, in Bilbao. That's where his factories are."

Duran motioned for Bernardo to continue.

"Father was choking her. The gun went off. He fell down by the desk."

"The office door was open?"

"No. It was shut. I opened it and saw them. He was trying to kill her, Inspector."

"This wasn't the first time he'd beaten her?"

"God, no." Bernardo's eyes flashed bitterly.

"And this gun. Did you know about it?"

"Yes, she showed it to me when I was home last. Father gave it to her. He was a fanatic about protection."

Duran pursed his lips, probably restraining himself from noting the irony in Bernardo's remark.

"What did you do next?"

"I took the gun away from her. She was hysterical."

"One last thing. Did your mother usually keep her handbag in your father's office?"

"I don't think so. She had it with her when she went to talk to him. He wanted to see some sales receipts. They were in her purse."

"Why did he want to see the receipts?"

"He found out about a bill for some furniture. That's what set him off. It was usually something like that, especially when he was drinking."

Fortunately for us, Esteban *had* been drinking, apparently about half a liter of wine.

"One moment." Cervantes raised his hand for the interview to pause while he caught up.

Duran nodded and studied the painting of the monastery behind Baroja's desk.

"There won't be any problem, will there, Inspector?" Bernardo said. "My mother's already told you all of this. She's devastated. But it was self-defense. After all these years of putting up with it."

"I wouldn't worry, Brother." Duran waved away Bernardo's fears with his well manicured hand. "Your mother has not been charged with anything. As I said, this inquest is a formality, a requirement of the law."

Duran questioned me for a few minutes. Why was I at the Esteban house? Why did I arrive after Bernardo? What did I see? I spit out everything I'd agreed on with Bernardo and his mother. Bernardo and I traveled to Madrid together, but on the way to the Estebans I'd decided to go back to a vendor and get white roses for Señora Esteban. Bernardo said she liked them. Then I remembered I had no money and walked to the house. I knew Baroja was probably

pissed about our little trip together, but, considering everything, I wasn't too worried. When Duran asked if I'd ever
witnessed any abusive behavior on the part of Esteban, I
just about called the inspector an asshole. But I checked
myself and promised him that Señora Esteban had not bat-
tered her own face. Duran clearly didn't care for the
remark. Just to push my buttons again, I'm sure, he asked
me why Señora Esteban had never contacted the police
when her husband hit her.

"This is Spain, Inspector. And she's a Spanish wife.
Bernardo advised her to report him. She refused."

"Is that so, Brother Bernardo?"

Bernardo nodded.

Duran wrapped up the interview. Bernardo and I went to
our own cells, his fucking idea, not mine. I was restless as hell,
pissed at him and wanting his ass worse than I'd ever wanted
it, probably because I couldn't have it, at least not now.

It was my own fault. I'd told him the truth, every fucking detail of it. It was on Good Friday night. He'd come to
my cell, sobbed in my arms. I stroked him, kissed him,
made long and slow love to him. When I fucked him I wanted to merge with him. I wanted him to take me, body and
soul. I almost cried afterward. My throat got tight. I could-
n't say a word or I'd break down, so I locked my arms
around him and lay there in the dark without opening my
mouth. Then, as though someone tripped a switch inside
me, my heart pounded like a jackhammer and the words
rushed up. I told him everything—why I came to Santo
Domingo, how I killed Castro and saw his father kill
Entralgo, the letters, everything. I promised him that I had
tried to stop him in the end—that part was true, that *was*

why I'd followed him to Madrid. When I started, he lay dead still. Then he tried to break away from my hold. But I fought him, made him stay until I'd finished. Then I let go of him, but he stayed in the bed, limp, paralyzed, like someone who'd fallen from a rooftop.

"*Dios, Dios, Dios,*" he whispered without moving a muscle.

"I swear to you Bernardo. I swear I love you. I was wrong. I used you. But I swear, I love you. You're the only thing I want in the world."

He shook his head. "It's too much. It's too much."

"Forgive me." I'd never said those words before in my life. "Please."

"Shut up! Shut up!" he shouted.

I let him. What else could I do? What else could I say?

He got out of the bed. Fumbling, he got into his habit and left.

He didn't talk to me the rest of the weekend. Then, about an hour before Duran's interview on Monday afternoon, he came to my cell. He was cold as a nun. Determined. Fortified. He'd probably come straight from the confessional or some fit of mystical ecstasy in the chapel.

"Baroja's agreed to ordain me," he said. He stood by the door. Like he was prepared to escape my advances if I made any. I got up from my desk and sat on the bed to face him.

"And that's what you want more than anything." I didn't say "more than me," but he knew what I meant.

"It's what I've wanted my whole life."

"At what price, Bernardo?" I had no right to be bitter, but I was.

"Funny question, coming from you."

I shrugged. "Do what you want. Get ordained. Consummate your little fantasy. Then I'll take you away."

His eyes softened.

"I'm an expert at waiting. So do what you want. Enjoy the great day. Then stare at these fucking walls for a few years, spend your evenings with Diego and old Jaime and Arturo. Oh, and Cristo, your true lover. See if he gets you off the way I do. It may be one hell of a dark night of the soul, Bernardo. For both of us. But I'll wait for you."

• • •

That week old Simon died in his bed at 6 o'clock in the morning. He seemed to time his death to coincide with my arrival at Santiago for morning mass. The hysterical housekeeper met me at the door and directed me upstairs, where she'd looked in on the priest and found him struggling to breathe. I retrieved my stole and a vial of consecrated oil and anointed the sour-smelling old man. He seemed to recognize me. He closed his eyes while I read the prayers, opened them briefly when I'd finished, and then closed them again forever.

The funeral was sparsely attended. A torrential spring rain kept people away. I presided at the funeral mass, along with Father Cirilo Ortega, an oily-browed, bespectacled man appointed pastor of Santiago immediately following Simon's death. Apparently the Archdiocese of Toledo had requested my assistance for another decrepit pastor, but Baroja had other plans for me. He'd learned about a vacancy in one of the Salesian churches at Salamanca and negotiated the position for me. I later found out that Baroja recommended Bernardo for the diocesan position.

After saying my goodbyes to a few grateful parishioners, I hoisted my umbrella and walked to the mosque. Under its shelter I watched the rain through a keyhole shaped window. The shower pounded the tile roofs. The darkened sky had activated the streetlights, which dotted the gray panorama below me. And so it was over. Did I feel satisfaction? Maybe. Not as much for balancing the scales as for finishing a task.

I had a strange fear that my parents would recede into the shadowy margins of my thoughts. What could I replace them with? I could strike out now in new directions, leave monasteries behind forever. Why not? I was young. But why hurry? I was used to waiting. I could bide my time and wait for Bernardo in Salamanca as well as anywhere.

Twenty-Two

BERNARDO

My eyes went to the red. The archbishop's red chasuble. The red drapings on the altar and pulpit. The sprays of red carnations on either side of the looming reredos. Red. In the six weeks after it happened, I couldn't see red without thinking of his blood, the circle of it on his white shirt growing larger like a blossoming flower, spilling over onto the marble tiles, trailing along the grout and disappearing under his desk. Even on that day. Pentecost. My ordination. The moment I had lived for. Even then the blood came. Maybe it always would. Maybe blood was my inheritance. But it was also my Beloved's, whomever that was. Juan

Ramón's inheritance certainly. He'd been baptized in the blood of his parents and in the blood he himself had shed. And the inheritance of the Lover he had somehow merged with now. For I would never long for Cristo again without seeing the face of Juan Ramón. Cristo, crucified but triumphant. And triumphant I would be too. In one way or another.

For those six weeks before my ordination, the scene played itself over and over in my mind. It still does, months later, but not nearly as much. I see myself walking through the salon to the olive wood box, carved with roses and ivy. I see myself opening the lid, picking up the compact pistol. *Like a little metallic animal*, I'd thought, *curled up and sleeping*. I see myself lifting it gingerly, releasing the safety catch, then, in a daze, no longer needing to think or make decisions since all that was behind me, advancing to his office. *Ave Maria, Ave Maria, Ave Maria*—an *ave* sounded in my mind with each breath I took. Was it for strength? For comfort? Was it a consecration? Maybe I prayed for all of that. Perhaps I even felt the breath of God moving me toward him, steeling me with his fiery spirit to violate the conventions of religion, to ignore my heart of flesh and defend the life of one in danger against a murderer, the annihilator of an entire family.

Afterward, I doubted my motives, of course. Afterward, I wondered if deep within me I suspected that Juan Ramón had lied and that he'd killed those men himself. And did I have selfish motives? Of course. I wanted to prove the lengths to which I was willing to go for Juan Ramón. I wanted to prove the depth of my love. The act would be a kind of consummation. Juan Ramón and I would be joined in the blood we had shed. Our bond, begun in blood, would be perfectly consecrated in blood.

At my father's office door I hesitated, but not from second thoughts. I heard him talking, barking orders on the phone. If I proceeded, there would be a kind of witness. I went in anyway, the gun behind my back. He glanced up, held up his finger for me to wait, turned, and hung up the phone. In that instant, I pressed the barrel to his white shirt. The starch made it crisp, like an altar linen, but the flesh was soft beneath. And his heart seemed to beat directly beneath that soft flesh, although the gun was at his back. It seemed to make the barrel vibrate. It seemed to be warning him, so I fired. He hit the desk hard, then slid down, pulling the phone receiver with him.

Guilt did come. In fact, very quickly afterward, when my mother ran down from her bedroom, when she recoiled at the sight of his body—the blood—then touched my face, my chest, becoming hysterical as though she thought I'd been shot instead of my father. And there was guilt later, when I imagined again the man who had scooped me from the ocean's grasp. And when the word *patricide* first sounded in my mind and I thought of Absalom's plot against his father David and David's tears. I confessed to a priest, who went dumb he was so shocked, and then told me I must turn myself in. But his absolution was not conditional. It can't be. From the moment I left the confessional, guilt, except in fleeting moments, vanished.

So my temptation immediately afterward to forget about ordination had nothing to do with guilt. It was as though my deed transformed me already into another, higher being and I no longer needed the mystical change that ordination would bring. I even thought that maybe all along I'd only wanted priesthood to escape my father or hurt my father. I'd destroyed these motives the moment I pulled the trigger.

Then Juan Ramón told me the truth. He'd used me.

Yes, I believed him when he said he still loved me, or at least I hoped it was the truth. But I wanted to hurt him. I wanted to show him that I could live without him, that I could live for Cristo alone.

And then there was my mother. How could I crush her by giving up ordination? After everything, she deserved to finally see this day. "I did it," she'd said, when Juan Ramón came into the office and got her to stop sobbing. "It was self-defense, Bernardo. They'll never prosecute me. Don't contradict me." And of course her confession was perfect. Juan Ramón encouraged it and so did I.

I spread out on the cold chapel floor during the invocation of saints. Young, visiting monks chanted the names in strong, haunting voices. *Santa Teresa, San Juan de la Cruz, Los Santos Angeles...* I felt the spirits of the saints hover over me like the Pentecostal flames described in the epistle. My forehead against the red cushion, I closed my eyes and tears dropped to the slates beneath me. The day had come. After so many years. After so much pain. The day had finally come.

And when I knelt before the archbishop and felt his hands pressed against the crown of my head, I closed my eyes to shut out his red chasuble, to shut out anything but the wafting incense, the *Veni Creator* chanted so prayerfully, the image of holy tears I imagined on my mother's face in that moment. Then, as I remained kneeling, each priest present filed past me to share the archbishop's consecration. One set of hands made me open my eyes and they fell on Juan Ramón's beautiful feet, like a Roman centurion's in their sandals. My impulse was to rise and take him in my arms. I drew in a breath and felt his hands and wished with my whole heart that they could linger there.

When it came time to be robed in the chasuble from the cathedral treasury, my spiritual director, not Juan Ramón, performed the honors. But during the vesting I caught sight of Juan Ramón's face. He was smiling.

He was still smiling after the ceremony, when he came up to congratulate me back in the sacristy before I went out to my reception. The voices of guests echoed through the chapel as they exited. The other priests around me were changing their vestments.

"See," he said. "Nothing to worry about. You're a priest."

I nodded. "When do you go to Salamanca?"

"This afternoon. I'm leaving the cat with Diego. He likes her."

Since Good Friday I'd avoided him, and he'd left me alone. I'd been caught up in all the preparations for ordination. And I'd spent the last week on retreat in Madrid. But in the back of my mind, the dread of this moment had never left me.

"I meant what I said, Bernardo. I'll wait."

Don't leave me, I wanted to say. *Please don't leave me!* But I kept quiet. I watched him wind his way through the crowd of priests and disappear. Then I uttered what only a year before I would have considered a sacrilege. Now, transformed by Juan Ramón, transformed by everything between us, I saw that what I said expressed a new vision of God. A God mysterious beyond understanding. A God not static, but ever changing, full of surprises. "Nothing is irrevocable," I whispered to myself. "Not even this day."